RAINING RUM

RAINING RUM

and Other Short Stories to Drink to . . .

Bobbo Jetmundsen

Bobbo Publishing
ATLANTA, GEORGIA

This book is a work of fiction. Names, characters, places and events are products of the author's imagination or are used fictitiously. Any resemblance to actual events, locations or persons, living or deceased, is purely coincidental. We assume no responsibility for errors, inaccuracies, omissions, or any inconsistency herein.

First printing 2004

ISBN 0-9743069-3-2
LCCN 2003095359

ATTENTION CORPORATIONS, UNIVERSITIES, COLLEGES, AND PROFESSIONAL ORGANIZATIONS: Quantity discounts are available on bulk purchases of this book for educational, gift purposes, or as premiums for increasing magazine subscriptions or renewals. Special books or book excerpts can also be created to fit specific needs. For information, please contact Bobbo Publishing, P.O. Box 550028, Atlanta, GA 30355.

DEDICATION

To my mother

TABLE OF CONTENTS

Foreword ix

Acknowledgments xi

Introduction 1

Holy Olive, Popeye 5

Good Impressions Are Funny Things 8

Son of a. . . Baptist 13

Fjord Lost 17

Down the Bayou 25

High on the Hog 26

Mamas, Don't Let Your
Babies Grow Up 30

Sauté the Jubilee 33

Amongst Decay 37

Shoot the Women First 38

Some Yankees Jez Don't Know 41

Red Sky at Night 44

Palms Away 46

Stockbrokers Don't Make
Good Waiters . . . Either 52

Take a Hike, Bitch 55

My Buddies 57

Piano Man, Paris 58

Polyester and Prose 63

Testing One, Two, Three 65

No Conditional Waivers 71

Herd South for Winter 75

Mad Drag Queen 88

Whoa, Nellie 91

The Naked Girl Needs Help 97

Where the Desert Meets the Sea 101

Wait Listed 102

Life? Close, but No Cigar 110

Worn Out 112

Pocket Full of Lira 113

Coat Check—Two Bucks 120

After Omaha 123

Raining Rum 126

Preacher, I Need a Doctor 130

He Went to Paris (Finally) 135

Iron Man 136

Tale by the Sea 146

Is He Available? 154

Down on the Dog 159

Abigail's Fairy Tale 160

Margole's Maiden Voyage 163

Out to Sea 168

About the Author 169

FOREWORD

Bobbo Jetmundsen has been in my life for years. It's almost too formal calling him a friend, for he feels more like family.

Our history dates back to the Alabama Dry Docks where my husband and I worked for over 30 years. It was Bobbo's first job out of college. From the beginning I recognized a special flare in the young man's eye—the same colorful light possessed by all three of my own children. I took him under my wing.

We have been flying high ever since, sharing zest and zeal for life and living from Key West, Florida, to Paris, France.

Once again, Bobbo pleasantly entertains me with another chapter in his lively story . . . one I've greatly enjoyed taking part in.

Cheers to *Raining Rum!*

> Loraine "Peets" Buffett
> Point Clear, Alabama
> August 31, 2003

My dear friend Peets died on September 25, 2003, having lived a wonderful life. We will all miss her. I've described her before as *inspiration in person*, and if you ever met her, you'd certainly agree.

To Laurie, Jimmy, Lucy and your families, I hope her lovely few words here touch you as they do me.

ACKNOWLEDGMENTS

Professor William L. Daniels, now retired from the English Department at Rhodes College, had us writing short stories for his class and he liked reading mine. Thanks, Bill, for your inspiration.

Many thanks to Colin Mathews for his patience and help in taking the handwritten stories and putting them into typewritten form. He had fantastic suggestions for ways the stories might be edited, and was a pleasure to work with. His own talented writing interests are varied...but just ask him about automobiles and you'll learn his passion.

Also, thanks to my assistant, Pedja Arandjelovic, for his help working with About Books, Inc., to transform these stories into a book.

Thanks to my clients for being so faithful to me over the years and allowing me this wonderful lifestyle. Thanks for being my friends, too. Finally, thanks to all my friends who tolerate me, and my abundance of opinions, with style.

INTRODUCTION

Subjecting you to my creative side has certain elements of deception and surprise. Deception in that this might actually look like a real work of literature, and surprise in that I have taken time between travels to do something besides fight hangovers with Advil.

Looking at my collection of stories after so many years of scribbling them down is perplexing at best. Maybe some critic, somewhere, won't throw up reading them and will offer me a glimpse of direction for any future writings. However, I will more likely be advised to go directly to Bourbon Street to finish off my few remaining brain cells.

My oldest brother is a lawyer and a writer. His first book, *The Soulbane Strategem*, was a fantastic read and is still doing very well. He wrote it using C. S. Lewis' *The Screwtape Letters* for inspiration. And a sequel has just arrived! Well, C.S. would be proud of ol' Norman's book. My father certainly was. He wrote the book while working long hours at his fine Birmingham, Alabama, law firm, and occasionally helping his wife Kelli raise their three sons Taylor, Nelson and Jonathan. (Those boys, by the way, were born on the same day while I was fly fishing in Chile.) My youngest brother, Howard, is designing hardware for satellites, raising two boys—Norman and Bennett—with his wife, Sally. Brother John and his wife, Anne, have a boy named Henry and a *girl*, Abigail. Yes, there is a little girl amongst all those boys and she seems perfectly willing to be spoiled a little! Our father was an only son but my brothers, as you can tell, are doing well eliminating any concern with the proliferation of our family name. "Abigail's Fairy Tale" and "Margole's Maiden Voyage" were written just for Abby and are included in my short stories.

1

My father died a few short years ago and we all still miss him. His love for literature and prolific reading included an ability to recite poetry. He and mom joined me on a trip through Maine in 1990 and a beautiful harbor scene triggered a poem neither of us had ever heard him speak. I often wish he had done some writing of his own, but providing for us was his focus and he succeeded fully.

My mother is just the best, really. Laughing and enjoying moments with her family and friends bespeaks volumes about her. She never sent us off to school without a big breakfast and always had plenty of supper waiting on us when we got home. Cooking, raising four boys, a dog and a few exotic chickens on Dog River—the magical place we spent most of our early years—was a full-time job. She often says she worried about one of her sons, more than the others, when my friends query her about me. I always enjoy hearing the serious tone of her voice as she tells them that, but the matter-of-fact nature of her comment is always mitigated by the ever-present twinkle in her eye as she lets out her signature happy sigh. My favorite dessert is her blackberry cobbler, which just barely nudges out her pecan pie. She would pick blackberries in the summer, hide them in the freezer until my birthday, in February, when she'd surprise me with that cobbler topped with candles.

My travels have ended me up in some pretty interesting places. Bob Hardin, a longtime friend in Tampa, calls me "shameless." Apparently he thinks inviting myself to all sorts of exotic places, nice homes and exciting events is weird. Another friend, from Long Island, once described me as "the guy who has never met a guest room he didn't know." I do prefer to stay with friends instead of a boring hotel, at least, most of the time. However, with friends like mine I certainly don't always have to invite myself. I have been fortunate to be invited often to go fishing, to the beach or, simply, to a nice dinner. You'd be wise not to forget my disclaimer: "Don't invite me if you're afraid I'll show up!"

This collection of short stories encompasses a wandering imagination of on-the-road experiences from my travels. My experiences are buried in the characters and places I've written about. I had no motive to publish them when I started writing but, after many years of them piling up in a drawer, I decided to get them typed up and here they are (a novel is still in the drawer!). I guess if I were younger, I might be diagnosed with ADD but, at my age, I just admit to having a tiny attention span and to have attempted to convey emotion in a short period of time. I'd suppose anyone on the go today would find reading short stories easier than tackling a big novel. Looking for something to read in the guest rooms I frequent before I go to sleep is often satisfied with a *very* old magazine. Looking over the titles of the short stories, I can see the countryside of France where "planting teenagers" during WWII is discussed in "After Omaha." I don't think anyone who visits there will leave without being emotionally moved, as I was. I wrote to my father while there, and said something like "I'm glad you aren't here." If you've never been to the Southern marshes, I hope you might be able to imagine the smell of the mud and the sound of the mullet jumping after reading the several stories of coastal places that inspire many of us. I have wandered through an olive orchard in Italy, watched the customs of the Mississippi delta residents, heard the honking of taxis in NYC and sailed the Caribbean. Those experiences have inspired the stories I've written for various unknown reasons. I've dreamt of beating the house in Vegas, just the way my character Wally does in "Is He Available?"

This book is intended to appeal to those who can tolerate the perspective of a Southerner attempting to appeal to the various senses and emotions of everyone. And yes, you'll find an occasional remembrance of our racial past. Heaven knows this isn't a travel publication but, in a tiny way, it might be close . . . it may even inspire you to travel to Rome to see the statue of Saint Bruno or go sailing on Mobile Bay!

Fair Play

Before you criticize my verse,
Show me that yours isn't worse!

Grace M. Kittrell
May 1926 – March 2003

Holy Olive, Popeye

Antonio married a wild older woman with hair that poked out of the top of her head. They met at the beach during the summer, while separately vacationing with friends on the Amalfi Coast. Antonio was in love right away—and still is. Henrietta never was—and still ain't.

Antonio's friend, Eduardo, just shrugs his big broad shoulders when asked about those two. The expressions that go along with those shrugs aren't to be missed, as they are humorous to anyone catching him in the act. To some, Eduardo's display was the only redeeming quality that wild woman ever had.

"She's not a real bad person," her grandmother was overheard saying. But that doesn't explain why she constantly let the air out of Antonio's truck tires. "She has an unusual way of being creative," the wild woman's older brother once said of her. Henrietta often described her older sibling as "dumber than an olive."

Henrietta, happily, is a clean person. In fact, she wears gloves when she lets the air out of Antonio's tires. Her constant bathing required Antonio to install another water heater so he too could take a warm bath. To her, hygiene wasn't limited to her outward body. The internal cleansing was no less creative than the outer.

Eduardo quit visiting them because Henrietta once made him wash his feet. That was on Antonio's last birthday when she opted to cook lasagna with anchovies. Antonio not only dislikes anchovies, he gags thinking about them. She claimed she thought he'd never notice them. That would be like a Mississippi tornado not noticing a trailer park.

5

Henrietta never worked in one place too long, but did so well in school that her intellect opened door after door when she did decide to take a job. Her working was a good thing, not the least being she'd usually quit letting the air out of Antonio's tires so he could drive her to work.

No one wants Antonio and Henrietta to have children, except Antonio. He doesn't bring up the subject often, because it usually gets her to start sleeping at her mother's. Her mother gets mad at Antonio, and the rest of the family is upset if mom's upset.

Henrietta had not been to confession since she was married but, with her father ill, she went to pray at the church, light a candle and confess. That young priest never knew what was coming when Henrietta scooted over to the little window that day. Clergy 101 probably touched on some of the possibilities, clergy 201 had a story or two and 301 was some serious stuff. For him, that confession was somewhere between a sky dive and an exorcism, which ended up with Henrietta joining a convent way up in the Umbrian countryside. She was there seven months before her mother sent for her to be with her father as he was failing in health.

Antonio was there to comfort the family during their grieving. Henrietta spoke to him in Latin then, which of course he didn't understand a bit. He wasn't sure whether she was coming to their home with him after the service. She did not. Antonio promised to keep writing her, though she never responded unless it was with Pope-authorized pamphlet propaganda.

Eduardo's wife basically adopted Antonio into their family. They did many things together and got along just fine, especially with their children. When word came that Henrietta had become *Sister* Henrietta, it was made clear to Antonio that he could remarry and he did. Sister Henrietta sent a cross as a gift for their wedding, along with some recycled candles. She also sent a note to Eduardo's wife thanking her for all she had done for Antonio. That gesture took the Sister out of the penalty box Eduardo had put her in for years. Her Mother Superior must have been glad to have her cleaning up the convent, her wild hair contained with her holy chapeau.

A few years went by, then it finally happened. Sister Henrietta is no longer at the convent. The episode of her departure, although under intense Sister secrecy, went something like this:

Mother Superior was praying in the courtyard, as is usual on Sunday evenings. Sister Henrietta was cleaning up when a storm rolled in and leaves began blowing everywhere. Sis H was chasing the leaves as they blew into the convent, but the air currents were swirling so and the leaves elusive. As the storm neared a particularly strong, and incredibly precise, gust of wind blew her into 10 rows of lit candles. How the candles remained burning with all that wind has many talking about divine intervention and the like. Then, her veil and hair on fire, the hot wax had her flying around like a moth trying to land on a light bulb. What those nuns saw and heard can only be imagined. Most would agree the devil had gotten hold of her. With her wild hair smoldering, her clothes smoking and nuns chasing her, she darted around until they caught her and drug her, screaming, to the holy water fountain. Those nuns nearly drowned her, holding her head under the water. Surely that thought entered at least one of those pure minds.

Henrietta was sent to some Vatican-sponsored religious rehab property where monks can assess her—she only speaks in tongues now. Antonio worries they'll perform an unnecessary ritual on her, as he has heard her do that before. Who knows, maybe they should.

Good Impressions Are Funny Things

"Sho-z hot, Mizta Reed. Adlanna be a lon' way n' dis," said Reginald Monroe, perspiring heavily while guiding the two-horse wagon south along Cartersville Road toward Atlanta.

"Yes, it's too far to get there today. Why don't we set up camp along the river somewhere? It'll be cool there," said Robert Reed as he, too, wiped the moisture from his dusty face.

Reginald and Robert had made this trip many times together. Reginald's family worked many years with Mr. Reed, an attorney and Kentucky farmer. Reginald's aunt raised Robert Reed and his brother as their nanny. Slavery was not a bad life for some Negroes. That is, for those who were free to think and, some, even leave.

"No, I think we should make Kennesaw Mountain. There's a trail up there and it should cool us off just fine. We'll wash in the streams before going up," Robert said softly.

Reginald smiled. He had often thought of climbing the very small mountain and looking out over the treetops. This was to be a real adventure, or at least a simple vacation. The beautiful mountain had caught the eye of many travelers for years. And it was a special place to Reginald.

"Down there, Reginald. What's that down there?"

"Looks to be a howze. Yes suh, why dats a howze."

"We'll set up camp here, then, and have a view of that place and the sunset."

"Dat be nice, da breeze sho feelz good. Yez, dat breeze—umm."
Reginald began to hum some music, familiar combinations of soul and
gospel. The melodies were both happy and sad, as he unloaded the
wagon and set up camp. The day was old, but summer nights came late
and the sun was still high.

"Where's my scope, Reginald?" asked Robert, who wanted his brass
telescope to peer about the surrounding area. Their campsite was in a
clearing that gave good visibility from the lonely mountain, about a
half-day from Atlanta.

"There's a white-haired old man. Down there. Look at his nice place.
There are fruit trees and rows of corn. The cabin looks empty, otherwise," said Robert, squinting one eye and looking through the lens.

"No chilluns?"

"No, but there are some big birds in the yard. Must be turkeys—
but they've long necks. Wonder . . . he's feeding them! They are running
up to him. Here, look!"

Reginald rarely was offered the delicate eyepiece. He took it from
Mr. Reed like a woman takes her newborn baby. His big, worn hands
were gentle and steady. He looked down the mountain into the yard.
"Gooses, Mistuh Reed. Dems gooses!" he said.

"Geese? Are you sure? Maybe you're right, by George. They may
be."

"Lots of fine things. Yez, it be nize."

The sun drifted a bit further down, and a blue-gray haze started to
form. Reginald started a small fire to heat some food and boil water for
tea. Robert loved his tea, quite a delicacy since it came from New York
only once a year.

"Dat corn looks good. Tall 'n green. Lez see, by Jule-lye. Bezt be
pickin' soon," Reginald commented as Mr. Reed looked down at the
farmer.

"He's sittin' down now, and the geese are headed down to the pond.
There looks to be someone coming to visit. Yes, it's a man and woman
in a small carriage. They're coming to visit him. It's nice to have visitors—company can get tiresome, but I like visitors."

The sun was in their eyes now. Their westerly view of the countryside was filled with spectacular sights. The air was cooling even though

the breeze seemed to subside. The white-haired gentleman greeted his guests and they took seats on the front lawn of the house overlooking the small pond. The sun continued its fall, until it nestled into the crevice of a gray cloud. Streams of rays extended upward, toward Kennesaw Mountain, and the edge of the big cloud was brilliant, showing its many features as it began to hide the sun.

With many overhead colors, Robert again peered with his telescope down at the farmhouse. Reginald unwrapped the tea leaves. After measuring the water, he dropped the leaves into the pan and held it near the coals of the fire to let it simmer for just a short while.

"He's really entertaining his guests down there," Robert said softly. "He's holding his hand outward with his elbow on the arm of the chair and fingers spread and talking quite deliberately. Almost looks like my friend Loagie Montrose."

"Ah don't know a Mistuh Montroze," Reginald said, straining the tea from the pot. He took the cup over to Mr. Reed quite casually, without even a ripple of tea.

"Ahh, Mr. Monroe. Thank you," Robert said and leaned back in the oak. "Loagie was in law school with me in Virginia. He could charm a raging bull, that fellow. He would put his big hand out in front of his face, distracting your attention as he looked into your eyes. Look down there and see what I mean," he said handing Reginald the telescope.

Reginald took a long time looking around. He scanned the house, the barn, then the corn, peach trees and pond. He, too, saw the old man talking to his guests.

"I sees a menz fishin'," he said. "Looks at him catch'n fishes!" he exclaimed as he watched a black man on the bank of the pond catch a fish. The white-haired gentleman walked down to the pond where the fisherman was and put his hand on his shoulder. The black man was smiling and Reginald could see he was happy to be there.

"Sposin' dey's eatin' fishes tonite," Reginald said as he laid the telescope down on its silk cover.

Robert was enjoying his tea as Reginald took some food from the fire and fixed a plate for himself. "We'll eat better tomorrow. I hope so anyway," Robert said as he looked down at the food. Reginald would wait until he was finished, killing time by tending to the horses, as they were a bit unsettled standing on the uneven ground.

"Mo tea?"

"Not now, Reginald," Robert said and put down his empty plate."

"That was as fine a supper as I can ask for, Reginald," he said letting Reginald know he was finished and it would be OK for him to eat.

As darkness began to set in, the gray surroundings were welcomed by loud chirping crickets and an occasional distant, groaning bullfrog. The lightning bugs flew around and a few mosquitos snuck out, attracted to the light of the lantern.

Dinner was over down at the farmhouse as the guests were getting in their carriage for their twilight ride home. "Must live close by. Hell, its damn near dark!" Robert mumbled, peeping one last time through his lens.

The smoldering fire sent a layer of smoke out over the air which lingered and surrounded the treetops like it would never go away. The faint smell of the pine and oak burning was almost sweet.

Robert and Reginald were preparing to sleep. The peaceful night in Georgia was beginning. The next day wasn't far away. The lantern was still on and it was totally dark outside their camp. Lightning bugs still blinked their lights. The farm below had disappeared into the darkness.

They arrived in Atlanta around noon the following day and went to the Atlantan Hotel to clean up before Robert's business appointment.

Reginald waited down in front of the hotel for Robert, and was busy looking at the city, its people and the merchandise in the store windows. No one paid any attention to Reginald, even though, in Kentucky, his carriage usually caught glances from passersby.

"Reginald, it's too hot to sit outside, you should've come inside," Robert said as they headed down Peachtree Street.

"Sho'nuff hot. Da horsez a bit hot, too," he said.

"Well, drop me off and go straight to the stable. Leave the carriage and walk back to meet me here," Robert instructed as they stopped in front of the law offices of John Shelby.

Reginald walked up Peachtree from the stable. It was quite dusty in the heat and his face was covered with beads of perspiration. It had taken about an hour to get back to meet Mr. Reed. As he entered the front door, he could hear the attorneys in conference. The doors and windows were open with little circulation and Reginald sat on the wooden bench against the foyer wall.

He could hear one of the attorneys explaining how their client could in no way be expected to do business with Mr. Reed's client without a signed agreement, which would be beneficial to both parties. Another gentleman took the conversation a bit further, standing and raising his voice to dramatize the fact that they didn't need a Kentucky business partner anyway.

Reginald watched as Mr. Reed sat in his chair across the table from the attorneys and their client. He was silent. The lawyers continued their speaking until the older, well-dressed man with a cigar said, "Mr. Reed, just what do you have to say to us?" interrupting the lawyers' dissertations.

Robert Reed eased back in his chair. Reginald was on the edge of his bench, holding his hat between his knees with his wet hands. The length of silence caused the others to look at each other. Finally, he raised his right forearm up, resting his elbow on the corner arm of the chair by the table. He spread his stretched fingers and moved his hand just enough to his left to look past the back of his hand into their eyes.

"Gentlemen," he pushed his hand forward, "if I thought we were coming to Atlanta to draw up a bunch of promises, I'd a stayed in Kentucky. The Stillman family I represent was looking to do business with you to hopefully make a tidy profit for everyone. They have my respect and have lived up to everything they've ever agreed to." He laid his hand down on the table. "I'm afraid the type of business you are suggesting is a bit too complicated for us. I'm quite sorry to have to put you to any trouble to be here and respect your courtesy for inviting me to visit." With that he stood up, said goodbye as he shook their hands and walked toward Reginald. They were about to leave when a voice said "Robert . . . " They looked back and it was the gentleman with his cigar.

"Can you, and your friend, come to my house for dinner?"

Robert Reed looked at Reginald Monroe, then turned to him and said, "We would like that very much." And as they walked out of the building, Robert put his hand on Reginald's shoulder and a smile came across both of their faces.

Son of a . . . Baptist

Angie didn't really give a crap about the fact that her ex-boyfriend was moving back to the neighborhood with his new girlfriend, a model who gets into the glossy pages of low-class glamour magazines. "She look like she's . . . well, a slut is putting it nicely," she thought when she heard news of their pending move. What she did care about was that he still owed her some furniture he'd absconded with that hot summer night he slipped away from her house in Inman Park . . . her fathers house, no less. Father had never known the asshole boyfriend ever lived there. It had been kept secret from dad—he grew up the son of a Baptist preacher and as long as Grandpaw was alive, well, you can go figure. In any case, her dad had been the need for covert habitation.

After six months, it finally happened at an art gallery pushing African crafts. He was gulping down cheap wine like the freeloader he was, and little miss slut was posing with her plastic wine glass like it was Baccarat. The thought of her with all that expensive makeup, given to her by the caseload, was enough to dial 911.

"So, Henry, how've you been?"

"Not bad, Angie. Let me introduce you to Chrissian . . . darling, this is my old friend Angie."

The runwayish turn was almost evil as she, in fairly good stead, twisted her head and torso in such a rehearsed move so as to need to tilt her plastic wine glass to prevent the liquid from spilling on poor ol' Henry's silk Hawaiian shirt. "Probably fakes her orgasms with the ex. I know his equipment couldn't work for that woman. And, that name of hers! You can just see her twirling her stripper-like body on stage with dollar bills folded into her garter," she thought to herself.

Chrissian twirled away to feed arrogance to some hanger-on, wannabe asshole—the type who frequent events like this even when not invited. The back of her head was more acceptable anyway.

Inman Park is an old neighborhood of the bygone era of small town Atlanta. It was home to turn-of-the-century Southern elite, who entertained in grand style; with their porches and hanging electric fans moving the humid air, allowing the fine cotton attire to be appropriately cool. Pretenders replaced the elite. The pretenders vacated for the suburbs and were happily replaced by hippies. The hippies wallered around the big houses smoking pot, burning incense, cooking mushrooms and managing their trust funds. They matured, cut their hair and replaced themselves. No one is exactly sure just who lives there now. The grandeur of the past resonates here and it has maintained an identity, unlike the trendy midtown area it borders where, likely, the highest big-man-with-little-dog population in the world is found.

Angie's preaching grandpaw was the son of one of the fringe elite who had lived in a cute cottage with a big magnolia tree, which is still alive. For Halloween, they always hung ghosts from the tree for children to see when they came to the door for treats. Being an urban woman, she didn't even bother with the homeless who slept in her yard. That's just the way of inner-city living—the less fortunate touching the former aristocracy of Atlanta in their own style. Angie could deal with that distraction much easier than she could her new stripper slut neighbor. Oh the look of that bitch . . . not even acceptable in the neighborhood where anything goes.

Cleaning gutters seems to be a year-round need in Atlanta, where the variety of trees must be greater than anywhere else, and no one wants to plant water oak because it takes so long to grow. This is the era of instant gratification. Hanging black people from the big oak was instant enough. Now that such horrible behavior has subsided, only to be remembered by the images on display at the King Center, the gutters are full and in need of attention. The constant falling of stuff can secretly convert inner-city tree huggers into chain saw owners. They only affect themselves and the returns department at Home Depot a month later when they take it back still in the box, exchanging it for a leaf blower to move those fallen leaves into the streets, closer to their property lines, begging their neighbors to do something about them.

That oak tree stands strong, that dead black boy dangles, punished by hate, but getting mild revenge now as his image hangs framed, on display, in the realization of how inexcusable those perpetrators' actions, and the untold acceptance by their peers for those horrid actions, really were. Those pictures speak volumes, and the leaves from that tree would still be falling if the developers had not bulldozed it for a subdivision.

Angie climbed down from the ladder and went inside to go to the attic and look in some of the other boxes, which, until now, she'd been afraid to look through. She found some letters. And then, the folder she almost knew was there all along lay there in front of her. The heat of the attic and the stench of old mothballs didn't make a difference as she read them.

The ladder leaned on her gutter for a month. Finally, Henry came over and started cleaning the gutters for her. After all, he had done that chore for her before, and he did owe her money. She came home one day to clean gutters and a neatly raked yard. She cringed at the thought that Henry mustered up the courage and thoughtfulness to commit such an act, but could tell by the way the bags of trash were neatly tied and placed in Henryesque fashion on the side of the street knowing a call to thank him would be the appropriate action to take. She even had some nice words for the makeup maiden, should she answer the phone. Instead, she left a sweet message on their machine and thanked God for that outcome. She would bake a cobbler for him, since her peach recipe was well received in their live-in days. Forgiveness, it had been distracting her lately and it felt good to thank someone and somewhat forgive them at the same time. Cheap as it was, it felt good . . . real good, in fact. Negative thoughts are viral and hard to cure and she decided to work on a self-prescribed fix for those in her head. Fixing the Henry hate was easy. The slut would be harder, since she was sleeping with her ex and, for some reason, that really bothered her. Having them over for dinner was a solution, but the fact that she'd be just bullshitting everyone by trying to act civil just wasn't going to fly anytime soon. Maybe, just maybe, she could ask Grandpaw during her next visit to the home.

His mind wasn't what it used to be, and her expectation he could help wasn't high.

How could she have known that day, sitting outside under the tree at the convalescent home, several lives would be changed forever by asking her 88-year-old grandfather, the retired Baptist preacher with an uncertain past revealed from files forgotten in an attic, how to really learn to forgive. The breeze singing through the leaves of that shade tree harmonized a confession to God that went like this: "Dear God, your promise through Jesus is to forgive us of our confessed sins. However, from what I have done, I cannot expect forgiveness. I ask you to know that I am sorry and know that I deserve your toughest persecution."

Angie quit her job at the public relations firm to travel, teaching adult Sunday school classes around the Southeastern states. Her neighbors kept her house looking alive as her message called her beyond those bounds. Her grandfather's picture was placed over her piano, a symbol of her forgiveness of his past.

Angie returned from a trip to a note for her to contact a furniture refinishing guy. She recognized his name, from the many times she'd passed his shop on Piedmont Road near Buckhead, and called him. He wanted to deliver her coffee table he had been working on, ever since her friend Henry had paid him to restore it, saying, "I'm sorry it took so long."

Fjord Lost

The streets in the centrum were still very damp from the last shower. Crowds moved down the shopping streets and a musician played for coins as the afternoon wore on. Every two feet there was a place to have a drink of choice. After a while, your legs tire, soon after, you find yourself in the pub swirling on a stool.

Mark and Iris lived in the same apartment ever since they married, about a year ago now. The four-room space rented for a handsome number of guilders. Amsterdam is not cheap. Their furnishings were a mixture of new and used pieces. Their walls were covered with colorful paintings, mostly abstract with surprisingly similar styles, eye-capturing and giving warmth and personality to their home. Oscar, their dog, didn't seem to mind the visitors who would come to admire the collection of her brother's art, most of which he'd painted especially for her.

Eric had become popular among the art auction houses after giving in to his sister's persistent urging to paint. The many early works she saved seemed to be the only ones to have survived his moves to New York, Santa Fe (briefly) and Paris. Who knows, maybe some lucky collector would stumble across one of those early pieces he'd used to pay his landlord and fill up his Jeep with gas.

Eric's father never understood art. His mother confided to him that his father would occasionally look at the color photographs of his works in books that had been published, but to expect him to grasp the concept of splashing paint on a canvas and find some appreciation was asking too much.

Eric had showings at a couple of galleries in the U.S. and asked his parents to make the trip with him. They were delighted to take the trip and see some of America.

A warm reception awaited them at every stop. Eric spoke casually to collectors and met curators for breakfast to help them better understand his work. This allowed him the luxury of visiting their museums without tourists. His father asked to join him on one occasion and Eric could detect his liking for some of the magnificent landscape paintings. He especially favored some of the Norwegian fjords, probably because he had traveled the fjords as a young naval cadet aboard the Startsborg Lemkuhle, a large old sailing ship used for training in Bergen, Norway.

Criticism of Eric due to one painting, his recent work depicting two women in a sexual scene with each other, was the topic most curators brought up. His abstract style was being compromised, they said. His explanation, "My intention was to simply express love. There are many ways to do this, and these two are good at the message of love." The curators frequently responded, "Yes, but what you intended and what is commonly being interpreted are different then. How does that make you feel?" Juan Rombrada asked this very question. He was the assistant curator of Chicago's Ferguson Collection, and one of the larger collectors of Eric's work.

"I feel just fine," said Eric in a less-than-convincing tone. The exhausting tour schedule didn't help him during difficult periods of questioning. He wasn't accustomed to being on the defensive in his work, and it portrayed him as a deer hunter staring at a big buck in the woods.

"What might we expect from you next?" Juan inquired, surely insinuating any additional depictions of this type of art could damage the market for his works. Fighting anger, Eric felt the curator had crossed the line. He thought for a long minute before he responded. In that minute, he decided if he was to be devoted to himself as an artist, he must not be pushed too much to maintain the integrity of his past works at the expense of his future. He had known this time would come for him, and he took it as a sign of opportunity. To be forced into that compromise, which so many artists accepted throughout history, was never a consideration for Eric. He made more decisions during that pause than in all his years of mixing colors on canvas, depicting thought and emotion.

"Landscapes," Eric finally said.

"Excuse me?"

"Land . . . scapes," Eric annunciated. This threw Juan off and he closed his book of notes.

"Thank you for coming by today," was his curt response. He collected his belongings and walked Eric to the door.

As Eric walked with his father across the parking lot, his father began to create conversation with, "So what if he's . . . he seemed not very . . . well, as far as I'm concerned, he can go fuck himself." This unexpected response started Eric chuckling, then outright laughing. That's when they decided to go for a beer.

After a couple of large drafts, Eric called to cancel dinner with a private collector from Canada, Lars Hansen, who had flown in for a showing.

Lars got the message and called Eric's suite at the hotel to inquire about the reason. "He's exhausted and decided to have a couple of beers with his father," his mother responded on the line.

"Where are they now?" Hansen asked.

"Don't know," she said while thinking, "they didn't say."

Lars knew a good bit about Eric and thought he might go to Marla's, a small establishment near the warehouse district. Painters often went there during the day. It was an inspirational spot. He walked in the small foyer and could hear music leaking from inside—Johnny Cash. The large painting of the old dock area on the wall behind the varnished teak bar was well lit. Reflections caused a nice amount of light to fall on the few people listening to the growling singer as they spent the afternoon getting tipsy.

Mr. Hansen had not been to a pub like this in a long while. He felt uncomfortable at first, but not as much as if he'd worn his tie. Eric wasn't there. He found a small area with a tiny sofa and a couple of chairs. A waiter looked over from the bar as he was wiping out glasses from the washer. "Dewars and soda," he hollered. After a while, in the warm peacefulness of the place, he quietly ordered another. He took out his cellular phone and set it on the table, after checking the strength of the signal from inside Marla's brick walls. He asked the waiter for a glass of water and a cigar, if they had them.

"You know, we don't carry cigars but I just happen to have one and you're welcome to it," the waiter said as he went to retrieve it from his locker.

The waiter handed Lars the Churchill-sized smoke. "Don Diego was an early favorite of mine. Thank you," he said as he began licking the dried tobacco wrapper. Kindness like this didn't happen in the uppity places Lars usually found himself in. After several puffs, he relaxed into the sofa and smiled at his personal thoughts. "Here I am, worth a bunch of dollars, in a place none of my friends or colleagues would dare go. I've got a limo driver, asleep for sure, waiting outside to take me to my table at Spiagia. So many people would've been keen to be my dinner companion, but I'll go alone it seems. It's too good a break to not have some personal time."

"Sir, would you care for Armanac? We happen to have some that belongs to a customer of mine. He would be happy for you to have a glass."

"Absolutely. What's your name?"

"Alfred," he said.

"Go for it, Alfred," he said with his slight accent. Alfred only thinks he's likely to get a nice tip. Certainly, he'll be surprised. Lars is having more fun than he has in many years. Halfway through the cigar and some lovely tastes of the Armanac, as Aretha sang about a telephone ringing, he called his driver who said the restaurant had called to get an update on his intentions. "Tell them I don't know," he said, slightly irritated at the restaurant for being so inquisitive and attempting to put him on a schedule.

He looked up and saw an older man standing near the front door looking as if he either owned the place or had never been there. Lars stayed curiously aware of him. Moments later, he saw a couple entering. It was an older woman with a younger man. It was Eric, escorting his mother, and the gentleman near the front door followed them to a table. Eric sat down between his parents and Lars watched as the three enjoyed each other. Eric's father stood up to look at, and admire, the painting of the harbor. Eric watched as he looked it over, and Lars observed his mother making a comment to him privately.

Eric stood up, walked over to his father and began explaining the painting. His father shook his head and began commenting about something. Lars watched as Eric listened, smiled and patted his father on the back.

Lars called his driver. "Did you see the three people who walked in about 15 minutes ago?"

"Yes, sir."

"How did they arrive?"

"Taxi."

After thinking for a moment, he said, "When they are leaving I will call you. Pick them up. The younger fellow is Eric Hoghton. Take them to Spiagia if they are hungry. Just don't tell them I'm inside here— you're clever enough—make something up." His words were cut short by the blare of a country singer who sang about three words, two hearts and one night together.

After almost an hour, the Hoghtons got up to leave. Lars hit send on the phone and said, "Here they come."

The driver pulled the black Cadillac limo up front. As they walked out, he opened the back door. "Mr. Hoghton?" he said, "I'm here for you . . . and these must be your . . ."

"Yes, my parents."

"No one knows we're here," Eric said.

"It was just a hunch on someone's part," the driver said.

"Who?"

"Well, let's see . . . while I'm not particularly instructed to withhold that information, I'd prefer to deliver you to dinner. Are you hungry?"

"Yes," his father blurted out. They all laughed.

"Spiagia?" the driver asked.

"Lars did this," Eric said, with no response from the driver. "Was that him smoking the cigar in there? I'll go see . . . please, everyone sit in the car a minute."

Eric walked in and found Lars on the sofa, puffing the last of the Don Diego. "You haven't been here all the while?" Eric asked Lars, who looked just slightly startled.

"Hello, Eric," said Lars. "I came here when your mother said you were out for a beer and, yes, I've been admiring you and your parents."

"Dad's hungry. Are you still free for dinner?"

"Oh, you three go. I'm enjoying myself. Really."

"No, Lars, we need to talk. I'm glad this has worked out."

At dinner, Eric explained the conversation at the Ferguson Collection and how he didn't want to compromise his work. But, after his two women drew so much criticism, his career was in possible jeopardy. Lars listened intently. He had planned a similar conversation with Eric, as had Rombrada. "How foolish of me," Lars thought to himself.

"What did you say to that?" Lars asked when he heard that Juan asked of his future intentions. Eric looked at him with a slight twinkle and said, "Landscapes." Lars looked at him as if he were serious, and then thought he must be joking. He raised his wine glass to Eric's parents and said, "Here's to landscapes," and wouldn't give Eric any hint of his true thoughts.

Eric wondered to himself, "Surely he doesn't think I'm serious." He toasted "skol," in honor of Lars' Norwegian heritage and, with that, Eric's father and Lars were talking about Norway for the rest of the dinner.

Back home in Amsterdam, auction houses, including Christie's and Sotheby's, began calling Eric to ask questions. Evidently, the Ferguson Collection was planning to sell a large group of his work in the fall sale.

Eric responded with his usual, "I'm not sure why they wanted them in the first place." And, as might be expected, the prices for Eric's work plummeted when buyers were scarce and no reserve had been placed on the works. A range of expectations between $50,000 and $100,000 produced no offers over $50,000, and they eventually sold for less than $30,000 each. Lars was suspected to be one of the buyers rumored to have acquired several pieces, although the buyers were mostly anonymous.

Critics started writing of a demise and Eric took it somewhat poorly. His latest works were placed at higher prices that surely would be reduced. Galleries called and he tried to explain that his goal was not shortsighted and he felt comfortable with the direction his career was going in. They were quite unhappy with him at first but, in the end, they went to bat for him by calling their best clients and creating renewed interest.

Eric initiated a conference call for his favorite gallery owners and the customers they had nurtured. Confidentiality prohibited him from knowing who some of the buyers were, but this didn't faze him. After his commentary, he asked for questions.

"This is Gerbard Strong. My question: Since we're to expect a new style, have you named any of the latest works?" Gerbard had sold several of Eric's paintings to clients and owned one himself.

"Well, yes," Eric responded. "But it's not for sale," letting everyone know that nobody on the call was the potential owner. "*Fjord Lost* is the name." Silence. More silence.

Fjord Lost was for his father. The arts community asked for pictures. They were denied. It was a private matter for the family. Several months later, Eric's first public showing of a new painting was held at a small studio in Amsterdam. The owner of first rights viewed the work, called *Harbor*. The price had been adjusted downward from $75,000 to $55,000. He bought it and would put it up for display at his corporate office. A new following began to develop, but buyers were still nervous.

A private tour of the work was arranged for Lars. He viewed it with great effort and asked some of his advisors their thoughts, for it was known the painting *Harbor* was for sale. The gallery put a range on it of $68,000 to $82,000, but the owner's price was an astonishing $125,000—net! Lars bought it.

Other works began to sell and, within two years, Eric was well accepted and adjusted to his new style. Then something interesting happened: a foreign buyer bid a million pounds in London for one of Iris's paintings, after a private viewing of her collection. A brilliant work, it was entitled *Fjord Lost*. She called Eric in tears. She and Mark could really use the money. In fact, Mark was furious with her for even thinking twice about it, but nothing would trouble her more than selling a painting which had been a gift from her loving father, who passed away the previous winter. "Sis!" Eric quipped, "You cash that check. Dad's spinning in his grave thinking you might not take the money. I'll personally throw Oscar out the window if you don't sell that damn painting."

Oscar's ears perked a bit. The painting was sold and the marriage saved, along with the dog.

The following frenzy of confusion among dealers made the front page of the art section of the *New York Times*. Eric was on his way to becoming one of the most successful painters of his time. The article was titled "Mind Your FatherScapes."

Down the Bayou

Once I met the motion of the waters, I found excitement.

Following my curiosity, I was led to shallows, beaches, canals and creeks. Adorned with overhanging limbs from bushes and fallen trees—even turtles, gulls or occasional pelicans—depending on where I was. They became my hosts and I was good company.

There were shadows on calm waters from the overhead clouds. There were rains on the waters, splashing. Colors changed as clarity, depth and light varied. Brackish waters held considerable life. Within the marshes and mud there were tiny birds with tall birds.

Places like these are made for thought. Long horizons and open spaces visually give the mind a finite panorama in an undefined existence.

I hope I can think of something important before it gets dark. Even then, I'll still hear splashing—for the mullet will be jumping tonight on the bayou.

High on the Hog

Owen Parsons was a farmer. He was supposed to be. After all, his father was. His wife's family were farmers. His schooling had prepared him for this career, considered one of the most difficult to predict. He grew cotton, soybeans and wheat, and would have a lot of pecan trees one day when he was nearer to retirement.

Through the county programs when he was young, he learned to interact well with people. He was often told he'd make a good politician. But Owen wasn't gonna do that—he'd just farm.

His wife helped bring social activities to their area. She'd gone off to college, one of those Virginia girls' schools. She said all she learned there was how to gossip about boys and smoke cigarettes. Truth was, she was very well liked, smart and had many friends.

With three children, the opening day of dove season was quite an event. Melissa, the youngest child and the only daughter, would entertain her friends at the shoot. Her good looks ensured some of the guys from college would certainly be coming to the shoot. They were usually placed in the field near each other, and her father enjoyed watching her dropping the birds at their feet with her skillful shooting acumen. The resulting damaged egos and denial gave them looks of tilted, shaken pinball machines.

Some farmers in those days lived quite high on the hog . . . long wooden fences along the highway leading up to the entry drive, shaded with rows of pecan trees and green grassy areas planted to please the eye. The Parsons, however, lived modestly knowing that having to pay the note on the place could be a burden at times. But there were good years, too. Those years of good harvest are when we learn more about people, not just farmers, by how they handle their successes. As the sign on the church said, "No matter how much money you have, you can not buy back the past."

The first year Owen had extra money was in the early 1970s. His boys were helping around the farm, having not been on a vacation for two summers, and his daughter was eager to go anywhere away from the Mississippi delta heat. Owen took the family to Florida to see Disney World. Instead of an Oriental rug for the den or an oil painting for the mantel, Owen had other thoughts. One being an anonymous gift to the church. Then there was a donation to the high school for new band uniforms.

Warren Potts Jr., a neighbor's son who had been very close to Owen, had left the farm country to live in Atlanta. Warren Jr. was known as Wally growing up and, against his mother's wishes, decided to keep the name. Wally had always been one of Owen's favorites, and they spent many hours together in a duck blind discussing duck blind politics.

The duck blinds are interesting pieces of property, situated in various locations within the fly zone of migratory ducks. Hunters brave usually quite cold mornings to get to those cramped quarters before the sun rises, when the ducks like to fly around looking for breakfast. Wearing waders, which will never be a part of anyone's look in fashion, trying to get just a little bit warmer; safely loading shotguns with the ever noticeable clicking of the magazine and slamming of the breech as three shells sit in waiting. All the while, making sure the reeds of camouflage have adequately covered the morning's selected place de deception and, at the same time, finishing the story you started telling when the truck heater finally thawed your toes on the way there. Duck blinds are no place for argument—after all, everyone has a loaded weapon. Duck hunters are all friends though, even if they have never met. Amazing resolutions to all types of issues are mulled over and discussed in those duck blinds, with the hopeful interruption of ducks flying overhead. Some quacking of the duck call, which is an art form in itself, often proves to be just enough of an enticement to get those beautiful birds to look your way and quack back. The dogs start whimpering in anticipation of the loud firing of guns and then the splashing of downed birds on the water. You know the dog is not cold, but damned if you know just why not.

Wally and Owen had enough hours in the duck blind together to know they shared similar opinions on life. They knew where they most likely disagreed, too, but duck blinding is not the venue for debate.

One Christmas, Wally told of his new business venture. Owen listened. He had seen the boy do things from fixing a tractor all night so it would be ready for the morning work, to personally driving a farmhand's sickly, elderly family member to the hospital. He always waited for report of their health with the family, for hours on end, if need be. Those workers would do back flips over bonfires for Wally.

Owen's investment in Wally's first venture was lost. Wally came to see Owen and explained the failure. Great product, poor markets and not enough of the right kind of marketing. Everyone lost their money. Owen understood and was more concerned for Wally's self-esteem and well-being than for himself and his loss. He encouraged Wally to keep his mind on the future, not the past, and to keep in touch with him about his plans.

Wally recalled, years later, the great confidence Owen instilled in him and placed that experience at the top of his list of reasons for his incredible success. Owen's subsequent investment in Wally would prove to be exceptional, as Wally had been able to acquire an established business from a family who felt he could make a difference and protect their employees, who had become family friends. They accepted Wally's proposal over several that were financially superior. Wally did not disappoint that family with his business judgment, and the trust he gained from his employees helped him successfully acquire other companies. Eventually, the investment banks convinced him to take his company public. Wally had become very well-known across the country even though, unlike many of his peers, he worked hard to keep a low profile.

Owen died one afternoon at home in his chair, watching the weather on television. He had not been feeling well for a few days and was fast approaching the prospect of being moved into an assisted living facility. His life was cheerfully being discussed in his crowded farmhouse, as friends and family converged to pay respects. His children were grown and their children listened intently to retellings of Owen's life stories when word spread Wally was driving up the driveway.

Wally had flown in from his home in New York. He walked in escorting his 88-year-old mother. The room was quieter. This home-town-boy-done-good was truly a celebrity with this crowd. Mrs. Parsons was seated in the living room with some of her friends, looking out of the picture window at the oaks and the bayou, as they approached. After the initial looks of grief passed, Mrs. Parsons asked them to have a seat and they talked about how much Owen loved the house and the farm.

After a while, Mrs. Parsons walked over to Owen's desk and lifted the oak cover from the top drawer. She picked up a letter and brought it back to where Wally and his mother were seated.

Holding Mrs. Potts' hand, Mrs. Parsons said, "Owen wrote this to you many years ago. He finished the letter in an afternoon, placed it in the desk, but never got the courage to give it to you." Her name was all that was on the sealed letter. Their many years of friendship were solidified with experiences from sharing committee duties at the church to helping each other pick out appropriate Christmas presents for the other's spouse.

Their friendship had proven unshakable through many years of life's challenges. Mrs. Potts and Wally began to wonder just what the nature of Owen's letter might be.

"He's probably writing to fix my cornbread recipe," she said, bringing a chuckle to the room. "But," she started as she slipped the letter into her purse, "I've not the courage to read it."

Mamas, Don't Let Your Babies Grow Up

Elrod Packett just celebrated his 81st birthday. His grandchildren call him PawPop. Elrod retired from the Scott Paper Company in Mobile. His wife passed away two years ago, and his only daughter lives just off of Old Shell Road with her husband and three children. He spent a lifetime spoiling his little girl.

Most (make that *all*) parents want their children to have a great upbringing, with grand experiences . . . good times, education, sports, more education with a dash of cultural exposure, jobs, families, church and financial success. Isn't this called growing up? Taking life seriously, but hey, you should be enjoying it too.

Children don't know about serious because they just start crying when serious shows up. They know a lot about cartoons, ice cream, junk food (ice cream is *not* junk food) and are darn good at being selfish. And because they can be so darn cute, they get away with the selfish thing easily. Pretty bows in little girls' hair and boys with clip-on ties at Easter are signs of cute prepared with a heaping tablespoon of innocence. To wipe cotton candy from a child's face is a little like cleaning up after a New Year's Eve party—the fun's over, but wow, was it worth it! To make a baby smile, ride a bicycle for the first time, drink your first chocolate shake at the counter of a diner (or drugstore, if you're ancient), catch a fish, see a rainbow, watch as someone plays a piano, get your first paycheck and to do real good at something you enjoy are all magnificent memories most of us have. Isn't it good to think back and realize how some of the simple ingredients of our upbringing are so memorable?

Elrod still loves his treats and, at his age, why not? His grandchildren smile when they hear he is coming to visit. They know there will be peppermint ice cream and cookies. They also know their mom and dad will enjoy him, too. Someday, someone will figure out that children learn from the laughter of their parents, likely even before birth. PawPop laughs a lot when he comes to visit, and so does everyone else.

PawPop speaks less seriously these days. He's lowered his guard since he doesn't feel he's got much more to teach anyone at this point. He's figured out some other things for himself, yet there are many things he says he's quit trying to figure out. This is not a sign of complacency or ignorance. For instance, he doesn't understand why the bream won't eat worms sometimes. He still wonders where people get all the money to live like they do down in Florida. He gets bored with the church figuring out who can belong, and can't believe anyone would eat out when they can cook a perfectly fine supper at home.

Some people have never seen the Christmas lights at Rockefeller Center. Some won't ever see Old Faithful or the Grand Canyon. Baseball records fall all the time, and some won't care if the Hammer's record ever gets broken, or who steals home plate the most.

Have you ever taken time to feed the pigeons? Look at old man Sylvestor feeding those birds in the square. That's not such a grown-up way to be, is it?

PawPop loved seeing Sylvestor. So did a lot of folks. But some just rushed through the park to be on their way, not even speaking to his inviting smile. Had they ever stopped, the man would've been worth listening to. But they had no time for it and, now that he's gone, they can't ever do it. Volumes upon volumes of interesting stuff never get recorded. You can't go rent *Stories of Sylvestor* to take to Gulf Shores for the weekend. They don't have a copy, only God does.

Chocolate chip cookies so fresh they bend. Flowers so pretty they glow. Stories so corny they're funny. Old clothes pressed so neat and clean they look stylish. A circling and erratic bat flying over the backyard at dark. The bell you ring with your thumb on your tricycle. Silly children with runny noses talking about nothing in particular. Honey on your hot buttered biscuit. A stock you made money on. A Girl Scout selling thin mints. Seeing your grandparents, their home and their friends. A hidden picture of an old flame. High school. First grade. Oh yeah, your first baseball game.

Oh, grow up. You don't want to read this crap do you? You probably think all environmentalists are kooks. Are you one of those people who drive all across town for the cheapest gas? You'd rather read about the rising cost of cereal, crowded airports and lost luggage, politics or the latest conspiracy theory in the tabloid. That's what affects a lot of us today, no time to dream. No time to visit. Besides that, pigeons are filthy anyway.

Sauté the Jubilee

The howling gusts of wind gave a cooling effect to the otherwise hot afternoon, which made for a good nap on the porch overlooking the bay. Edgar did not feel tired, but after a lull in activity and the slight ache of sleepy bones he settled in for a nice snorey nap. The trees moved when the wind passed, but Edgar awoke only when he heard the luffing of sails. He had a visitor from across the bay, his friend Willis, and what appeared to be a sorority of bikinis. He rubbed his eyes and when he looked up, the sails were being lowered along with the anchor. The *Sauté* was at rest just offshore of their pier.

"Edgar, is that Willis?"

"Yes, Ma'am."

"He said he might come over."

His mother looked over her reading glasses. "My word! He's brought the entire university with him."

"Oh, Mom . . . . his girlfriend from school is down on Dauphin Island with a few friends. I suppose the more the merrier?"

"Hope the water patrol doesn't stop him to count life jackets."

"Me neither, Mom."

Edgar and Willis were both college sophomores. Edgar was at Princeton, and Willis was at the University of Alabama. Willis' girlfriend, Jill, was a Kappa from Huntsville. Her father played for Bear, and all of her aunts and uncles attended the university at one point or another. Huntsville is a long way from Fairhope, Alabama, and the accent is, too. That accent is most like Tennessee, not like lower Alabama.

Willis' little brother Timmy would be a senior in high school next year and was more than happy to be his older brother's first mate for an afternoon of sailing on Mobile Bay. The girls found him cute and flirted with him constantly.

Edgar would be a hot item to them too. He was the placekicker for the Princeton football team, but looked more like the quarterback. He cut grass during the summer for extra money, and the labor kept him fit.

"Ho there!" he shouted as he stood on the end of the pier. "C'mon ashore!"

The girls were flustered. They didn't want to reveal their untanned bodies to someone they didn't know, but in order not to they would need to put on t-shirts—an option they were not particularly fond of either.

From the pier, Edgar wondered if something was wrong, but soon they were splashing into the bay like a bunch of coots with their heads bobbing just above the surface. Timmy was ahead of them and approached Edgar before the flock could arrive. "Hey E-Man!"

"You horny enough, Timmo?"

"Whew! Check out the one in the blue and white!"

Edgar carefully put his hands out in front of his chest (so as not to be seen by the oncoming sorority girls) looking for acknowledgment. Timmy responded with a bashful smile. "Huge!" he silently mouthed.

As they got closer, the pack of girls got tighter. Edgar started counting them and twice got a total of nine. The girl in the blue and white revealed herself as the waters began to shallow on their approach to the end of the pier. Mobile Bay is known for how shallow it can be, even a considerable distance off of the beach. Just enough horrible accidents resulting in neck injuries keep the locals warning visitors of that danger. Otherwise, about the worst thing that can happen is to be attacked by a stinging nettle while you float with your coozie of beer.

"You girls must be here under duress! Surely you aren't with Captain Willis of your own free will?" That line sounded just as bad to them as it does to you here. Men trying to be cute with women at first pass gives the female psyche plenty of anti-venom. Some guys never recover. Edgar would win them over—it was just a matter of time.

"How about a beer!" Willis shouted. Edgar responded by launching a Bud Light in his direction. It bounced off of his hands and hit a lone piling full of barnacles and began spewing like only a shaken beer can do.

College sorority girls have a sense of humor unlike anything much known in modern behavioral theory. The underage sipping of beer-induced, sun-soaked, away-from-the-parents, on-a-sailboat influence was a volatile combination that yearned for culmination in the most tangible ways. Much like the colors Matisse could get away with on his palette . . . or consider other forms of perfect simplicity like bleu cheese and Bordeaux wine, or a fine cigar and a glass of Armanac. Today we're dealing with some of the finest ingredients of fusion cuisine you can cook up in life. Girls, beers, boats. Use liberally. Stir occasionally.

The afternoon ticked away with more laughter than is usually permitted for white folks. Edgar's dad had come in from a day's work and was headed down the pier with a large ice-cold watermelon under his arm. The large melon must've weighed 15 pounds and its color was a perfect appliance green with beautiful white stripes. The refrigerator that kept it cold held all the summertime delicacies—honeydew, cantaloupe and, of course, flounders, crabs and shrimp. On the rare occasion of a jubilee, when the flounders and crabs wander ashore (you're reading this correctly, hang in there), that fridge fills up with the scooped-up and gigged delights.

Cleaning flounders is about as easy as fish cleaning gets and, with a big stringer in tow on a good night, a sober gigger can do well. Edgar's dad had experienced so many jubilees in his life, he'd become one of the better forecasters of the event among his friends and neighbors. He would teach you like this, "The conditions start with a later-in-the-afternoon cooling shower which creates a calming of the bay followed by an ever-so-slight easterly breeze. The elevation of the eastern shore protects the beach from any of that breeze touching the close-in waters, not even a slight ripple can happen for the conditions to be ideal."

"Dad, can I sail back with Willis and spend the night?" Edgar asked his dad as he was cutting the last of the watermelon and the final seeds were spit in a rapid-fire mode over the rail.

His father thought for a minute and responded, "Do you want to miss the jubilee?"

Edgar thought just a second, then knew the gusty breeze just wasn't part of that famous recipe. "Yeah, Dad, I think I'll sit this one out."

With that answer, his father grinned, signifying that his son's graceful maturing as a young adult met his approval—a smile only a father can deliver. And, at least a few of the Kappas seemed pleased, too!

Amongst Decay

A faint roar could be heard in the distance. As I walked toward the source, the sound continued to climb and it appeared the powerful noise would reveal itself just over the dune ahead. A fire burning provided light and warmth. Otherwise, it would be cold and dark.

Dead and dying being moved by the power, with the living happily going about their business. The lifeless now just debris of the past being washed into mounds of matter, or just being buried alone by the surge of the surf.

That roar constant, with the fire burning sun and the thick salty odor, inviting deep inhalations that fill your lungs with medicinal pleasure. You see some of the living ambushing their targets from standing positions, while others dive from up high. Justifiable homicide in their minds, otherwise it probably doesn't even occur.

I worship this place of death. Lessons taught here are often forgotten. The return here reminds you of the experience you've missed, for you had been where you could no longer hear its roar and smell its breath. All over the world are beaches like this, and I'm hopeful to know more of them before I lie there myself, scattered amongst decay.

Shoot the Women First

Carlos Sanchez toiled daily in a South American rubber factory. The Sanchez brothers grew up working in South American rubber factories, just as their father had. Carlos' brother Manuel left that life to start one of his own elsewhere.

Manuel never liked working. Yet, his new business was prospering and suddenly he had money. Manuel's business turned to the underworld and his friends were chaos. Manuel was never good to his wife. She couldn't leave him. The consequences were vicious.

Their wedding was the last glimpse at a happy man full of life, looking to build a family and enjoying a rich Latin life. What happened one afternoon at the harbor, with the hurried loading and unloading of rugged ships, would change Manuel forever.

Manuel had asserted himself in an unfortunate encounter on the pier one night and someone ended up dead. The altercation stirred a feeling of power deep inside this humble man; the stature he gained for killing one of the most efficient narcotics agents was too tempting to a man who'd always felt a silent, nagging need for fame. With his ears ringing from the wild praise of many who'd witnessed the incident, Manuel drifted helplessly to the darker side. His business of leading the trafficking of the South American drug trade quickly put him on various authorities' watch lists, mostly looking for payola.

The drug trade was bustling for Manuel and his wealth grew by staggering amounts. Carlos was certain of his brother's dealings; occasionally, Manual would boast of the money during rare appearances at family gatherings. Certainly, he'd be drinking excessively.

Carlos later spoke of his brother as a distant relative. Manuel blamed Carlos for his family's rebuff. In a drunken fit of anger, Manuel visited Carlos one Saturday. As his men held Carlos, Manuel cut off his brother's thumb in front of Carlos' children. Not even his own brother was immune from Manuel's descent into an evil world.

Manuel visited the highest political figures to create a professional aura about his "business." His threats, cloaked in the acceptance of government approval, became more real. People feared Manuel Sanchez, even his closest friends.

Manuel boarded a small ship late in September and headed to Peru. The crew of 10 was serious and intense. Manuel liked them, so they felt safe from his rage. The journey consisted of visits to various ports of call with wild parties of liquor, ganja and whores. Kidnapping prostitutes was common and some were thrown from the ship, alive, at sea.

From Peru, the ship headed to a secret port in the Orient. A group of men boarded from a launch one afternoon and a party began. Discussions were especially of drugs, weapons and money. Of course, their means began to get complicated when Manuel wanted to make a statement to the world. He sent a private plane into the side of the French Embassy in Hong Kong. His lieutenant's dying for the cause brought new fears of Manuel from international authorities. He had become one of the most feared terrorists, though he could never be directly connected to these acts.

A year of his escapades left a trail of blood the world over. When he was called the biggest "Punk Thug" by the U.S., he called his crime ring together and planned a response.

"We'll land during the night on the shore of the Island of St. Croix. Shoot the women first, then kill the men and children and return to the ship." His orders were final. One of his men voiced concerns about the plan and was promptly dropped from the bridge of the ship with a rope around his neck. He hung dead in open view for days.

The Panama Canal authorities were paid off handsomely. They would never acknowledge certain information of the passage of the ship that supposedly carried a cargo of canned tuna.

Once in the Caribbean, the ship steamed northeasterly. Manuel laughed often about his plans and their inevitable success.

One hundred miles from St. Croix, the captain radioed for some high-speed boats to meet the ship. Four boats were on their way, unaware of the horrible plan. Their skippers would be killed once aboard the ship.

It was mid-January—St. Croix's busy tourism season. Manuel's men were certain they would be undetected under cover of the heavy tourist traffic in the port. They loaded their weapons into the fast flotilla and headed to the island.

Carlos visited his mother when word of a terrorist attack in the Caribbean made news. Authorities reported casualties and blame was placed on Manuel Sanchez.

Maria Sanchez gathered her family and went to the church to pray, hoping for some understanding of what makes a person a villain. The priest blessed them and asked for the Lord to help end the bloodshed.

The U.S. Coast Guard and Mexican authorities, in a joint effort, quickly seized the ship. Manuel was not aboard. The secret service and CIA swarmed the islands. There was no word as the world eagerly awaited more information.

They'll find Manuel one day. For now he's in hiding, though some think he may have drowned. Those who knew him well don't believe that. Maria Sanchez fears her son is alive.

Three years later, Maria received a letter from someone who claimed she knew Manuel and that he was very ill from excessive drinking. Maria gave the letter to her priest and prayed for forgiveness in sending the letter to authorities.

The CIA in the U.S. analyzed the letter and felt it was authentic. They'll find him. When they do, it's doubtful he'll stand trial.

Only a mother can understand Maria's struggle, wanting her son to be stopped, yet, in some impossible way, be unharmed.

As the authorities closed in on Manuel, he, like other cowards before him, was found freshly dead from his own sword.

Some Yankees Jez Don't Know

Ottmer Walmsley wore wire rims. His overdone collegiate look transformed his jewelry-prone, fur-wearing wife into an easy target for some of the liberal extremist groups with spray paint. He grew up in Connecticut and, after a brief stint in Boston, took a position in Atlanta and the family moved to the Dunwoody area.

"I have, I want, give me, get this, I don't, let me, what's that . . ." Although moving in the South himself, Otty still looked at most Southerners as morons. He constantly chalked up his personal misfortunes to them and their region, saying, "That's the South for you."

Edward and Frances Ponder, a black couple from Carrolton, Georgia, had moved into a neighborhood near Tucker that was not too far from the Walmsley's new home. Edward was a jack-of-all-trades. He did yard work, washed cars, cleaned gutters, painted houses, bartended and even helped his wife with her babysitting. Francis worked for the city in the transportation department part-time and was in high demand to baby-sit, clean, serve parties and sing in the church choir on Sundays.

Otty was excited to meet the Ponders—he needed a lot of their services. The Ponders were enthusiastic about the opportunities Mr. Walmsley offered. He had several cars, a house, a wife and a baby.

Otty's cars were kept up nicely. His yard was never ignored and his baby never cried long when Frances took over. His wife's dinner parties went smoothly with the help of the Ponders.

"Hey Otty, how you doin' there in Atlanta? You eating grits yet?" his friend Ernie asked.

"No, but all I need now is a plantation! I'm getting to like the lifestyle of the south!" he said with a quite distracting fake Southern accent, giving his tone an underlying racist flavor.

Several months later things would change for Otty. He had to contract with a lawn service, take his car to the local detail shop and scrounge for young girls in the neighborhood to do the baby-sitting when they could.

The Ponders had moved on and it seemed no one would take their place. Though the Ponders were too polite to ever explain why they left the Walmsleys, don't think the neighbors were at a loss for gossip about the circumstances. From bridge game to garden club, the story about what actually happened was adequately being blown way out of proportion in most elegant Southern style.

One day, Mr. Coghburn came home early from work while Frances was cleaning his home. He didn't get to see her much due to his long hours, but he really enjoyed getting her input on the family and her perspective on whatever a person wanted to talk about.

"Frances, I understand you don't work with the Walmsleys anymore?" Mr. Coghburn half-stated, half-inquired.

"No, suh, we had to move on."

"Was there a problem?"

"Well Mista Co-burn," she said and paused. She hemmed and hawed enough to make an economist sound opinionated. Obviously nervous about figuring out just how to explain what had happened without letting the incident get Mr. Coghburn upset—which he surely would be if he heard the truth—had Frances moving her eyes from left to right in hopes of distracting him from her almost contrived answer. With a scowl she blurted, "Dem folks, Mr. C, dey jez don't knowz a good nig'ra when dey seez one!"

Mr. Coghburn was stunned and Frances quickly put her hand over her mouth. After staring at each other with wide eyes, the two burst into laughter. "Well, Frances you just let me know if you need some more work and I'm sure we can figure out something."

"Mista C, I'ze been thinkin' bout some mo work, but at some point 'dis old woman gonna have to slo down. I'ze don't need no mo Walmsleys in my life."

"You know, I've been thinking just along the same lines, Frances. It might be time to spend more time at the beach soon." Frances started smiling, because she had cherished the working vacations to St. Simon's Island with the Coghburns. Maybe if they spent more time there, she and Edward could find a way to do the same. The thought of this gave her heart a warm surge of happiness.

Red Sky at Night

All day at sea was the expectation of every enthusiastic guest and, with the weather outlook calling for near-perfect conditions for sailing, the captain ordered the sails raised. Wind is quartering the port side for a near-perfect beat southward. The leeward sides of the islands are calm, the gaps between the islands rougher. The boat's hull speed is about optimum in either environment.

Fishing boats here and there are doing their thing and we are gliding along our way. The music has turned classical all of a sudden and the blender is quiet. The faint smell of the captain's cigar—a cheap Cuban—swirls about.

The rigging sings, too. Stays and halyards all fight, popping and whistling as the wind makes them do. Bold construction from this Maine-built yacht gives comfort to all, though the seas are generally tame. The hull echoes the impacting chop.

Why does all of this make us happy? Are we just at peace with ourselves? The blue sky is red and gray now, and a reflective white tops the water. Ahead are the flashing reds and greens to direct this massive boat into port. There awaits a great restaurant and a bar full of people drinking. "If we can only avoid a hangover for the next day at sea," we think now that the lights from town are easily seen.

The mainsail comes down and is furled. The ginny pulls us ashore with a full-of-wind poise, giving the boat a graceful pace. The captain relights his cigar. His youngest son is his mate and is one step ahead of his father's orders. This makes our captain most proud.

The sky is bright red on the horizon, but the stars don't care. They are out anyway, welcoming the nighttime as the sun setting is all but done.

A small boat comes alongside. Gestures reveal old friends as the docking begins. Others watch us from their yachts, homes, bars and mopeds as we close our day of sailing. We are playing a substantial role in their beautiful Caribbean sunset experience.

A good breeze, great weather, perfect navigation and color . . . sprinkles of each give the day power in charging our souls. The powerful ambiance of nature is saturated upon us in doses of perfection.

What's missing? Did we forget something?

Probably not. But after a few Bombays I'm sure there will be an obvious oversight to this day. Will tomorrow be as great? Well, tomorrow will have its chance to be as great. Meanwhile, does anyone know where my sandals are? I'm goin' ashore for a cocktail.

Palms Away

A young man from Tennessee arrived in Key West with a smoldering spirit, damaged by his first marriage and all of its baggage. He resorted to listening to Jimmy Buffett records, drinking rum, reading all the books, then heading to the end of the road—a coastal island town with a particular personality that appealed to his tarnished pale soul. He had to establish a new life and this town of last resorts, also famous for large beginnings, opened its warm arms once again to take in another in need of the magic only the palms can shade.

"Hello, you're Mr. Hayworth, aren't you?" the newcomer said to the older man sitting on top of the coral wall in front of a church on Duvall Street.

"Who's Hayworth?" he asked, as if interested in really knowing.

"I've read your last two books and most of the articles you've published." He paused to see the convincing blush on Hayworth's face. "You spoke to a reporter once and said you learn from watching people in their routines each day. About four years ago, I wrote you a letter and your reply, with a flyer on your books, had Caroline Street as a return address. I saw you here when I first got to town."

"How long you been in Key West, uh . . . I don't know your name?"

"I'm Jerry. Jerry Welby."

"OK, Jerry, when did you get here?"

"Three months, sir."

"Welcome, Jerry."

"Thanks, Mr. Hayworth, I figured you wouldn't be upset if I said hello, but don't worry about me bothering you anymore. I just wanted to take the chance to say hello and thank you, or congratulate you likely is the better way of putting it, for your writing."

To experience Key West for the first time ranks up there with memorable firsts. Sometimes, many of your firsts happen in this southernmost cay. At any rate, there's the conch train to show you around and bars to cool you off as you look for Hemingway's house, and pass by the old library, the fort, the tarpon under the pier at night and the Green Parrot. Oh, that's a bar, not an animal. At least down there it is. Bahamas Village is even hip these days. Voodoo and all.

"Ruthie, a young man came up to me today and knew who I was." Carden Hayworth said to his wife of 35 years.

"That's number three in about three years!"

"Yes, and this is the first time it wasn't a woman my age looking for a suave novelist to sweep off his feet!"

She said, "I hope to meet him, too, sometime."

Summer was getting old now as some of the locals began to find cooler habitats. The Hayworths stayed the summer, hoping the ocean breeze would keep the temps from becoming extremely and unbearably hot. Construction crews are never out of work keeping paint on the beautiful old homes and replacing rotten wood pieces that moisture or termites (or both) have taken advantage of over the years. They come from all over to just be able to afford to get by. No 401(k) plan is necessary to get these beer-drinking workers to sign up for duty. They find their way to Schooners Wharf a little before quitting time and guzzle up some cold ones as the tourists look at them like they are supposed to be seen.

"Hey, Mr. Hayworth!" Jerry shouted as he biked by him on Simonton Street, headed to check out the lobster catch down by the boat ramp at the Hyatt. Hayworth just smiled and nodded with a tip of his cap, just like the pro golfers do when they make a putt.

Boats were tied to the pilings and folks sat around looking for nothing to do. Jerry took his chance, and sat on the opposite end of a bench from three men who seemed interesting enough to maybe befriend. "Did Miami win?" One of them asked him.

"I'm sorry, I don't know" Jerry said, disappointed he didn't know the answer.

"Seen many lobsters?" he asked them.

"Yup . . . a fair few," one of them answered. "Whar ya from?" he asked.

"Memphis."

"That's the place where they have those ribs . . . what's it called?"

"The Rendezvous," he said, a tad relieved to know the answer.

"Hell yea, that's fine food!" he said as one of the men walked away to stand in the water. With his feet in the wet sand, he propped his face toward the bright sun, letting the sun soak up last night's booze and parch his already not-so-smooth skin. Jerry watched him appear to be meditating, and decided to let him do his thing.

"Been down here long?" Jerry asked.

"'Bout an hour."

"I mean in Key West."

"Oh, fifteen years now. The wife's an artist and she keeps me busy making her picture frames. Don't bother me none havin'er making groceries," he said and turned to get on his bicycle. "See you 'round." Just like that, he went away. Jerry turned and the guy standing in the water was gone, too. He was alone now with paradise just teasing him to either get with it or not. He was determined to figure it out. The life he recently left was a vortex he didn't care to return to anytime soon.

Thanksgiving was a week away now and the reality of spending his first Thanksgiving alone was beginning to be obvious to Jerry. Emotional strength had been in order to just get here in the first place, but there were times like this when novelty wears thin and panic attempts to prevail. When his parents called him later in the day, he was very afraid they would ask of his plans for the holiday. His mother finessed the issue simply stating, "We all will miss you this week and hope you can find a piece of turkey all the way down there."

The day before Thanksgiving, he rode his bike to a pick-up job at the Pier House bar called the Chart Room. On the way, he stopped to get a Cuban espresso at Sandy's window on White Street and saw the special was a turkey Cuban sandwich. That was comforting to him because the chance to at least get some turkey tomorrow was paramount in his thoughts. Little did he know, the Hayworths had been looking for him to join them for Thanksgiving.

"I usually see Jerry, but I haven't seen him in several days. Gosh, I don't even remember his last name," Carden said to his wife. "Maybe it'll just be us after all."

"We could invite Simon, he has brought us fish all year and we never see him," Ruthie said.

"OK, Ruthie, I'll find Simon," Carden said.

On the way to the grocery, Ruthie remembered that Jerry had written to Carden. Since she kept all of the letters, she could find his letter and get his last name to at least see if the local directory had a listing. She found it, and it read:

Dear Mr. Hayworth,

I just finished your book Playing with Paradise, *and felt compelled to write and express how much it meant to me. Your character Jameston intrigued me seriously enough to want to someday feel what it's like to go with instinct and emotion without becoming possessed with selfishness. I hope to visit Key West sometime if it is as intoxicating as your stories portray.*

With best wishes,
Jerry Welby

Ruthie smiled after reading the letter and dialed 411. His answering machine answered and she left a verbal invitation to come to 474 Caroline Street around 2 o'clock to celebrate Thanksgiving with them.

Jerry worked a few extra hours at the hotel and headed for the Afterdeck Lounge at Louie's Backyard to see if Chris would pour him some martinis. After he had three, he ordered a fourth as the dinner crowd started to arrive in clean clothes and leather shoes. A couple girls from Miami moved closer to Jerry. He was drunk now and they were, too, with one standing facing him with her arms around his neck. He was absorbing all the attention he could. Soon, Jerry was in their rented Chrysler convertible heading to La Te Da.

Morning came and Jerry awoke in bed with a girl he only thought might be named Sheila. He was at the Marriott Mi Casa, a highly glitzy place for his taste. "Happy Thanksgiving, Jerry," Sheila said as he woke up. It was Thanksgiving, and he was sporting a fine hangover. He dressed in a blur, kissed her goodbye and walked to his bicycle. He rode home, took a shower and fell asleep. He woke up to the telephone ringing. It was his little brother, Howie, calling to see how his Thanksgiving was going. Only then did he notice his never-blinking message light was really blinking. After his conversation with his brother, he listened to sweet Mrs. Hayworth's message inviting him to have Thanksgiving with them. He jotted down their number, looked at the clock, rubbed his head, then dialed their number. After a bunch of rings, Mr. Hayworth answered.

"Mr. Hayworth, this is Jerry."

"Where the hell have you been?" he asked in a jovial tone.

"That's a story I'm not sure I can repeat!" he said.

"Well, save it. Come on over. Simon and his girlfriend just got here and are by the pool. I'm making the ice cream. We'll start when you get here, that is, if you can get here within the hour."

"Of course I can, I'll be right over," he said and they hung up.

Jerry looked for clean nicer clothes and got on his bike heading to the bakery for a key lime pie to take to the Hayworth's conch house behind a white picket fence. The lattice around the house held vines of flowers with blooms giving lots of color—bougainvillea, he thought it was called. The front door was open and he could hear music competing with his "Hello . . . I'm here," and he walked on into the kitchen.

"Mrs. Hayworth? I'm Jerry," he said.

"Hello, Jerry. How nice of you to bring a pie!" she said.

"Go out and introduce yourself to the others and I'll be ready to serve soon."

With that, Jerry went outside to the pool to meet Simon, a fishing guide, and his girlfriend, Diane, a bookkeeper.

Thanksgiving began and it was all about food, wine, conversation and new friends. Carden read some old Indian verse while they were drinking coffee. Before they knew it, they were saying goodbye and hugging each other. This afternoon had been one of the best Jerry had ever experienced. The newly created friendships made immediate plans to do other things, then Jerry was back on his bicycle . . . unstable, but moving in a direction that may as well be the right one. On his way home, he noticed his neighbor reading on his front porch. Leftovers in hand he walked up to the gate and said, "Hello, I'm Jerry. I live just across the street. I have some of the best leftovers from our Thanksgiving. You hungry?" Just as simple as that, he was sitting on the porch with a new friend.

"I'm Tom, and I'm starving. You must be an angel, not a neighbor!" Tom fixed his plate and a glass of wine for Jerry. The artwork in his apartment was incredible. They talked and Tom was explaining how he got to Key West when the phone rang. It was Tom's mother. "Well . . . happy Thanksgiving to you, Mom . . . yes, in fact I'm having mine right now with a friend," he said looking toward Jerry.

Soon, Jerry was at home in his bed watching the lights filter through the windows and the palm trees, as he thought about his new life. He surely fell into a deep Key West sleep, smiling.

Stockbrokers Don't Make Good Waiters ... Either

Having been given the "best" training in the business, the hotshot new broker at Merrill Lynch is pounding away on the phone in search of customers who will make him rich. He hasn't been there long and already the manager has fired four brokers who were not producing. Wall Street's formerly employed are spread all around us in their new endeavors. They can be found landscaping, selling copiers, dealing medical supplies, working for travel agents, guiding bird-watchers and even caddying on golf tours. But, where you will most likely find an ex-rookie broker (especially the incredibly pushy, hard-nosed former telephone jockeys) is at the side of your table, in the mahogany paneled restaurants, where you go to relax and enjoy a fine dinner with customers.

"Welcome to Carcass, gentlemen. If I can have a minute of your time, I'd like to start you with the wine list. You will find our selection quite deep and I can assist you if you have any questions. Since you will most likely be ordering steak or fish tonight, I'd strongly suggest that both a bottle of red and white wine be opened so they may begin breathing. For a good buy in the red, the '81 Haut-Brion is only $205 a bottle. It recently brought over $250 at an auction. I've been told we're about out of it, but I'm sure I can find some. Shall I secure one for you? You might want more than one, once you've tasted it!"

His name tag read "Hunter." He couldn't load a shotgun if he had to, had only seen quail on a restaurant menu and had never seen a real dirty pick-up truck in his life. He beamed a magnificent saccharine smile, his face glowing fresh from a stint in the tanning bed and left before we could even have the chance to react.

Meanwhile, we're left with a wine list when a couple of scotches would've been perfect. My next move is to flag down another waiter, who has no intention of noticing the napkin I'm waving like Old Glory in a gale. Finally, Rutherford, the waiter closest by, looks over as he's delivering a pile of fried squid to the table next to us hosting a bald guy with a beer gut so big he can't get close up to the table. I ask him if he could bring over a couple of scotch and sodas. "I'll tell your waiter," he sniffs and disappears into the crowd. They're definitely not into teamwork. One must be from Goldman and one from Morgan, we decided. My dinner guest and I have been friends for over 15 years, and we had tried several times to get together for golf, fishing or even lunch. Finally, we just picked this night over a month ago. So, here we are, about to start laughing about some of our friends as we update each other on their exploits.

Ten minutes later, Hunter brings out a bottle of '81 Haut-Brion and sets it on the table. "Look what I found! Shall I?" he asks, and we give the go-ahead thinking it might be the only chance we get to drink at all.

"We think we ordered a couple of scotches from your buddy Rutherford," I say.

"Great," he says, then he disappears, too.

He comes back ready to take our appetizer order. "We're out of the escargot, but have excellent crab cakes as an appetizer," he says.

I look on the menu and see they're $17.50, the most expensive of the lot. "What about our scotches?" I ask.

"The bartender had a rush and is a bit backed up. Let me go see what I can do," he replies quickly. The bar was empty, of course, but the perfunctory response—had it been true—would've been a good excuse.

We did get to order dinner and, when the food was delivered, the wine was poured and it all was delicious. Dinner ended sometime ago, and now the empty wine glasses are just in the way. The other dirty dishes are seemingly starting to grow mold. Catching Hunter's eye while I pointed to the ceiling was successful in getting his attention. He was chatting at another table—either former or future investors. We overheard him tell them in a grandiose tone that he was considering buying the place or opening one like it in Palm Beach, and then waltzed over to us like Mishka crossing the stage.

Laughing at the situation now, we visualized Rutherford and Hunter celebrating with their "Dom," dressed in their Hermes ties, discussing the positively certain direction the market is headed in after a profitable option trade earlier in the day. As for us, what we want is for the economy to pick up enough to give us some career waiters who want to deliver food and drinks to our table instead of hype, stress and sass. It was way too late to order dessert, "Bring us the check, Hunter. We're heading to the bar for a cognac." His 20% tip alone would be enough to feed a family of six at a Ryan's Steak House. But, rather than use our tip as a weapon, we opt to send him on his way just as his few retail brokerage customers had, and his manager, and his ex-wife.

The most important outcome of the meal was that two friends had good conversation and ended up planning a quail hunt in Thomasville, Georgia, the following week. We took some Haut-Brion with us, too.

Take a Hike, Bitch

Why the bus driver didn't stop the bus earlier and throw that woman off I'll never know. You see, she was trouble from the start and not many of us could even believe they let her get on in the first place. Wandering all around the terminal in Memphis waiting for boarding, nearly being run over by traffic, at one point she appeared to go behind some parked cars and squat. Maybe she was just doing some exercises, I thought. The alternative caused me nausea, as just about anyone could suspect what she was probably doing.

We finally began boarding the bus for Little Rock and my worst fear came true, as she was the first in line. It's interstate all the way and only a few hours drive, I told myself, keeping plenty of distance from the seat she appeared to be claiming. When the bus driver started the engine the action started and, before we crossed the river into Arkansas, it was getting worse. Everything from loud warnings ("It's a diesel engine!! A *diesel!!*") to panicked screams about traveling the wrong direction ("Little Rock is the other way!! The *other way!!*").

God only knows this woman's story. I tried to appear to be taking a nap, thinking to myself it would just get better. Then it happened. She took off one of her shoes and hurled it at the driver. It missed him and hit the front windshield. The interstate was busy, it was dark by then, and his swerving made the woman in front of me gasp. His stern look was wasted in the darkness. Her language at that point was mostly in tongues, with the exception of an extremely audible "asshole" repeated between chants. A few more miles down that boring stretch of highway nestled between soybean and cotton fields of Mississippi basin mud, she launched her other shoe with the velocity and tumbling form usually seen from an onside kick of a football. It banged around up front and he appeared to have recovered it without much damage.

Pulling over at the exit ahead, which had nothing but a stop sign and an arrow pointing to Horseshoe Lake, the bus driver carefully placed the right tires on the soft shoulder and turned on the emergency blinkers. That's all you could hear then, the clickitty-clack of the flashers. No one was stirring. With the emergency flashers clicking his every step, he moved toward her. Everyone was in suspense. He took her shoes and handed them to her. She immediately threw them back at him. He forcefully grabbed her. It was dark and I couldn't tell if he was gripping clothes, skin or hair. Dragging the hollering bitch to the front of the bus, he opened the doors and escorted her to the side of the road.

She was screaming louder now. He drug her into the soybean field. It was wet and dark. As he climbed back onto the bus, you could see mud on his clothes. He shut the door and radioed the dispatcher. They had the sheriff there in no time and, with her safely in the back of a car with her own driver, we were on our way.

We were on time to Little Rock despite the distraction. Volunteers lined up to give their accounts of the incident. I slept on the bench and waited for my bus to Hot Springs for the horse races. Friends and horse racing go together just fine, and I had saved up for weeks for this trip to meet some old high school buddies.

Not knowing much about the strategy of horse racing, I would find a tip sheet and a bag of peanuts to dine on while perusing the touts. I departed from the recommendation, however, in the third race. The horse I bet on was described as "wild from the gate to the finish, and totally unpredictable." The horse's name was Shoeless Sally. Instead of my usual $2 show bet, I bet $5 to win. With the incredible odds I got, I had second thoughts about that woman after cashing in the winning ticket for $130. I will always wonder, was her name Sally?

My Buddies

They're the phone numbers on the refrigerator and on the back of the phone book—your buddies. They go places with you and you meet them places. They aren't afraid to tell you how they feel and yet you're still interested to hear what they think. They ask you to be in, or attend, their weddings. They would rather hear from you than not, and you'd be upset if you weren't in touch.

You handle adversity better when a buddy is lending an ear. But be alone in a circumstance and the stress can get unbearable.

We are a part of our friends—an extension of their own personalities in a small significant way. We are better because of these people. And, our laughter? Well, it echoes in them, echoes in them, echoes in them.

Piano Man, Paris

"If I could play the piano, I'd make my debut in Paris." That backstreet sign was in front of a playhouse in a left-bank alley, not far from schools for young people. Wayne Pelligreen stared at that marquee, thinking about how amazing events brought him to France, from sleepy south Georgia, in the first place. He could still see Spanish moss growing over the dirt roads of old Skidaway Island when he closed his eyes, and when he opened them there were cobblestone streets of Paris inviting him to journey deeper into the culture of the City of Culinary Delight.

Wayne Pelligreen practiced the piano in Savannah until his father was transferred to south Florida. There he fished, suntanned with girls and drank 99¢ six-packs. His mother was ill with cancer and he helped her to die. Because she was so ill in the end, he was happy when she finally did go. She'd waited to hear him play the piano before she died, and all he could do was put together some chords on the old piano at the hospice. He wished he could play better for her, knowing she'd know the difference. But his audience was true, appreciative and proud.

When his father read the will to the children, Wayne sat and listened to his mother's humble wishes as to how her belongings would be distributed. She left him her two prints from Europe of a couple of churches. "Why'd she think I'd ever want those?" he thought. His sister wanted them. He almost traded, but they decided he should explore a bit and see if there might be a place, maybe even a reason, for them.

After graduating from college, Wayne decided not to pursue more formal education. Jobs, though, were scarce in Florida for English majors. He took a job at an insurance company in the benefits area; day in and day out he crunched numbers on stacks of papers. His first Christmas brought a bonus check for $2,800. He bought a new bicycle and an old piano for his small apartment. The remainder was paid to his credit card.

His friend Elizabeth played the piano with good form and precision. She never put much emotion in the pressing of the ivories, but could relate to Wayne and had patience with him. Their brief fling resulted in his learning to play much better than he'd hoped. Elizabeth moved on to date a computer programmer who was methodical in every way, Baptist and in love with shag carpet. Wayne opened a bottle of champagne when he heard they were engaged.

A week later, he smelled the strong odor of vinegar from the empty wine bottles in his garbage. "How pitiful and lazy," he thought, to not keep clean the remnants of his pale existence.

The next week at work, he pulled out his music book and began to look at stanzas from the hymnal at his church. His week began to progress into a weird mix of thought and music. He was glad his piano responded to his questions and his ear responded favorably to the sounds of the instrument. His hard work was yielding much more rhythm than ever before. The prints above his stereo came into focus and he suddenly had the strong desire to visit those locations himself. "Silly," Wayne thought to himself. He wanted to move there, not go for a vacation. They were the Church of Notre Dame and the Church of St. Germain in Paris calling him.

"Why would mother have these and why did she leave them to me?" Wayne began to read a whole bunch more into these than you can imagine. Maybe his mother had set him up. All along, he surmised, she hoped he'd fall for the idea of moving to Paris to practice the arts.

The weeks before he finally left were tense at times because his father had to advance him money for one thing or another. But, as his father drove him to the airport, he was less businesslike in his gestures and more excited, like a parent at a child's sporting event. As he pulled the last bag from the trunk and turned toward Wayne, his entire face was engulfed in emotion. His tears flowed uncontrollably. They hugged as Wayne held his confidence—he never felt like turning back. This conviction was confusion removed from emotion. Was it his mother's or his father's emotion urging him on?

Bartending at a piano bar in the Le Marais district was not as prosperous as he had thought, but when he got behind the piano to practice, people listened. He made friends. He partied a lot, too. And before long, a year had passed and his brother was coming to visit for Thanksgiving.

His younger brother brought a bottle of Wild Turkey and a big card signed by most of his friends. They enjoyed each other more than ever and suddenly Wayne knew his homesickness would not prevail over his purpose in Paris. He would stay here for the time being.

Two years later was the opening night for Wayne's first gig. A Parisian play had contracted him to a role where his skills as a piano player were going to be put to the real test. Wayne had not mentioned the opportunity to his family in Florida. What he didn't know was that his friends in Paris had notified his younger brother anyway. Parisians who knew Wayne called him the "Baby Banger," a sort of nice, off-the-wall French comment. That night was his night. His playing was superb, and the standing ovation turned wild when he walked out for a bow. It wasn't until after the play that he was surprised backstage by his entire family. His father was the center of attention for the entire week they were in Paris, and actually introduced Wayne to a cute French woman he'd met at the hotel. She would later become Wayne's wife.

The Baby Banger played with such vigor that he was invited to the opera in a tribute to a celebration of the Bastille. He was the only American performer, playing a melody based upon Southern American ritualistic slave music.

His wife, Toula, was from Nice, and they were blessed with two wonderful children. She'd met Wayne at the Piano Bar after his father had set it up after one of the performances. They often discussed the fact that he might want to move back to the United States. Wayne's creative energy waned after the next musical and he spoke to his two young children in English and explained how their new home in America might be different from life today. He'd been offered a job teaching music at Vanderbilt University in Nashville.

The family was no different from other families in the States. Their children went to college, worked part-time, and dated people Wayne hoped they wouldn't marry.

One afternoon he got a call from the hospital saying his son had been brought in for tests after fainting. The prognosis was that his son was terminally ill with bone cancer. Two months later, their son died at the age of 28.

To honor their son's last wishes, the family formed a plan to travel to France. The surprise to them was that his son had asked Father Sloan to set up a special mass for him at the Church in St. Germain, with his ashes to be spread in Nice.

Toula took the death very hard. She wanted answers from everyone from taxi drivers to bums on the metro. She wasn't sure why her son wanted to be buried in the south of France. He'd never lived there. The flat they shared when they were first married belonged to friends now, and they were celebrity guests for the many residents who knew of them from times past. Toula drank bourbon most of the night after the service in the flat near the Square Dumaine. She had turned up the stereo, playing a recorded reel-to-reel tape of one of her favorite concertos so loud that neighbors on the verge of complaining would inquire about the noise. When they learned of her son's recent death, all complaints ceased, and the mourning continued.

Wayne heard the piano concerto blaring on the stereo three blocks away on his way home from the wine store. He began to run as the music poured into the streets. His pace slowed and he stopped. He looked at the compassion of the silently standing crowd. As he stood there, he became aware that his mother never, to his recollection, cried in her life, yet there around him were ordinary mothers and fathers weeping tears of grief for the suffering of someone they didn't know.

He turned and walked away. Knowing his old piano bar was where his son's friends would be now. He walked away quickly so the sounds from his wife's stereo would drown into the warmth of the narrow streets, until the piano hanging over the doorway came into focus. Inside was a passionate group of patrons chattering and listening to music. He drank with his son's best friends and, when the piano became available, he took the bench. He began playing the famous piano pieces from the play that made him a legend in Paris years before. The music was well known in France still and, when word spread throughout the club that he was actually the lead from the original play and was playing the music, it seemed the entire bar had surrounded him to listen.

"How much more beautiful can the death of a mother and a son who never met be?" Wayne thought as he played for the appreciative and friendly crowd at the old piano bar. They sensed the exceptional energy of the guest pianist. If they only knew just a few of the reasons why . . .

Polyester and Prose

"The alleged incident appears to have occurred approximately in this vicinity around noon yesterday. The suspect is a white male and, presently, we are going under the assumption the individual acted alone. We have some leads in the case, but at this time we are not at liberty to discuss them."

Pot-bellied police have their own lingo, with sentence structure and thoughts that seem to resound repetitively across the country. It could be in Brooklyn, Detroit or in Saraland (a suburb south of Alabama). Watch the local news and you can hear their dialect in interviews from the scene. Have you heard it lately?

Why do we want to hear about the alleged? That's the media. Why don't we ever seem to hear what really happened? In the closing arguments of the trial, where the tone is quite different, where are the reporters? The defense says, "This man is not a criminal—he's a citizen like you and me who never had broken the law." Oh yeah? Then why did the witness observe the accused suspect entering the vandalized premises shortly before noon, slipping on a ski mask, while dressed in spandex tights?

"The prosecution rests their case on the testimony of a person wearing a ski mask. My client has never been skiing." So be it, but what about the tights? His drawers at home were full of them, but the jury never heard about that because the judge sided with the defense on relevance. If the judge would've allowed those details, maybe we'd have been able to learn more about the spandex collection. Did he do ballet? What about yoga? Hell hogwash, it's not relevant. How many citizens like you and me have a drawer full of spandex and look exactly like the person accused of the crime, picked out of a lineup by an eyewitness? Do you have to be a skier to wear a ski mask?

Oh well, I never considered law enforcement, or lawyering. And I've determined, since I don't like to wear polyester, I suppose that's a good thing.

Testing One, Two, Three

The river separated neighborhoods that were dissimilar in most ways. Several hundred yards divided people who worked in different areas and whose children attended different schools. Each listened to the other's dogs barking as sound carried over the calm water at night. It was a wonderful way to get along. They would wave at each other from boats during the summer days, and speak at the marina when buying fuel.

Mike Baker sat on the pier and listened to the band practicing across the river. The sound was good, some interesting new music along with some Dylan and Led Zeppelin. He wondered who they were and just where they practiced. Several weeks of Monday nights, the band practiced. Mike listened, for he loved and knew music. Next Monday afternoon, he'd ride across the river in his boat and see if he could listen in person.

"I'm Mike Baker from across the river," he said to the guys unloading drums from a truck. "I've heard you practicing and like your music a lot. Would it be OK for me to watch you practice?"

They looked at each other and shrugged their shoulders in indifference, signifying it was OK.

Not much conversation materialized, and Mike helped out only when it was the obvious thing to do. The guitars looked eager to be played. They were well preserved in their old cases. Soon, wires came from every direction snaking their way from here to there. Then the honking rasp as the speakers were fired up.

As they tuned instruments, they didn't even speak to each other. Mike's presence was being noticed. He picked up a magazine and started reading an article about how to name your band. Walter was closest to him. He held up the article and asked what their band's name was.

"Ain't got one," he said.

Mike looked lost with that and they smiled at him.

"One, two, three . . ." and the music started with a Cat Stevens song, after which Mike applauded and they said thank you in a concert sort of vocalic tone.

They talked about a new song for a while and played with some variations. Mike liked the lead guitar in one of the renditions much more than the others. He hoped they would ask his opinion, and they soon did.

"The other way, without question," he said. So, they pursued that direction and it got better and better. They ended with a chorus sung without the instruments, another suggestion from Mike, and it came together. They all felt good about the song and played it several more times.

They invited Mike back anytime. He yanked the starter rope on the outboard motor and headed home. Mike had football practice starting soon and he'd be late getting home. He knew he might not hear them again.

Football wasn't Mike's ultimate career but he was too good not to play. Actually, he didn't care much for the game. But the reality was, he was going to play. Sweating with a hard practice, he thought how nice it'd be to be sitting on the dock waiting for someone to pull him for a ski. That day, he decided to ski after practice—even if it was dark.

His brother Eric was waiting at home for him. "Eric, let's go ski," Mike said.

"Now? It's dark!"

"I don't care."

"Who's driving the boat?" Eric asked, for he never did that.

"You are."

"Me? . . . uh . . . " and he lit up!

"Let's go!"

As the hoist lowered the boat, Mike could hear music across the river. "That's weird, they usually practice on Monday. Today's not their usual day," Mike said to Eric.

"You listen to them?" Eric asked.

"Some. I watched them practice last fall."

"You want to hear something really weird?" Eric said.

"What?"

"For the last two or three weeks, they've been yelling for Mike across the river."

"Really?"

"I wondered if it was possible they knew you. But I just assumed it was a weird way of testing the microphone."

"Let's go over," Mike said.

As they pulled up to the dock, Mike thought about the fact that he couldn't remember all of their names, or even the name of the song he'd helped with. His little brother had never seen a live band. He also thought about how embarrassed he'd be if they didn't remember him.

"Hey, it's Mystery Mike," Paul said as they walked in.

"Man, you're real. We'd started to think you were a ghost," Walter said.

"How's it going?" Mike asked as he watched Eric looking at the sound system and reading stickers stuck on the speakers.

"Off and on is about it," Paul began. "We all liked your ideas and want you to help us out."

Mike just looked at them, puzzled.

"You are good," Walter said.

"OK, let me introduce y'all to my little brother Eric."

Mike then sat as they went through some of the new songs. Eric fetched a pen and paper for Mike and he made notes. Several new songs were great, and the band was maturing well together.

"OK, let me say this first. Y'all are sounding great. My taste is a bit different in a few areas of your music. I'm not sure if I'm a Motown addict or what, but I can't change some of your stuff—it doesn't strike me."

"We'll listen anyway. What do you think?" Paul asked.

"I want to hear you again before I say anything." And they planned a Sunday afternoon practice so as not to conflict with football. Eric wanted to come with Mike so badly that he felt obligated to bring him along.

After that session, Mike had quite a few pages of notes and they all gathered around.

"Walter, you're top of my list. You sing great harmony in the high-pitched octaves. I'm thinking you need some more chances to use that voice. Especially in "Margo's Cargo." Drop the loud guitar, Paul, and let him harmonize."

They discussed that idea some more and agreed to try it.

"Paul, you play great guitar, but you're making all of the songs sound alike. Soften it up and be more basic."

"He's right, Paul," Davy the drummer chimed in.

"Davy you need to pick up the beat in the two songs Paul sings with the acoustic—"Harlem Honey" and "Got Laid." It sounds too much like you bought it at Winn-Dixie."

"Wow, you're getting brutal," Davy laughed.

"Finally, Winston, you play some rhythm guitar with great emotion, and other times you're too bored to care. I hope you can at least fake it and get with it more 'cause your role in "Harbor Honey" makes that song."

After they digested the ideas, it was getting late and Mike grabbed Eric and headed out the door. Eric thanked his brother for taking him and drove the boat home.

Last they heard, the band had broken up. But many years later, Eric called Mike who lived in Spartanburg with his wife and two kids. It was about a new CD called *Mystery Mike* by a band called Raging Currents. They had become popular in the alternative rock circles. "Mike, go get their new CD and give me a call," Eric said. "Are those some of the guys from the river? Go get the CD and call me," he insisted.

Mike's wife, Deb, heard the conversation and said she had meant to get it. "Really?" he asked.

"You know, I have all of their CDs—*Troubled Wives* and *Laughter Not*," Deb responded.

"Damn right. I'd not paid attention. Wonder if Blockbuster has the new one?"

Deb immediately drove to see. Mike remembered being called Mystery Mike. That had been 18 years ago. It had never occurred to him that this new group sounded somewhat like those guys. "No, they are out of San Francisco . . . ," he mused, looking at one of Deb's CDs while she was still out. "Not good ol' boys from Mobile," he thought.

Deb returned triumphant with *Mystery Mike* in hand. The title cut was a song about a guy named Mike and his dedication to his little brother. Other songs included "Harlem Honey" and "Margo's Cargo." From the sound of it, "Margo's Cargo" was to be a big hit.

As they listened, Mike told Deb the story and dialed Eric. "Hey Eric, it is them."

"Yes, how'd you get it so fast?"

"Deb has all their CDs—she just went out and bought the latest one."

"Listen to it all and call me back."

Much to Mike's and Deb's amusement, their three-year-old daughter Melissa danced spastically to the album. After the last song, "Harlem Honey," Mike got up to turn off the stereo. Just before he did, the CD went to a hidden track and a voice said, "Eric, tell your brother to call us," followed by the sound of a guitar playing a couple of old chords from those years-old evening sessions.

The band insisted that Mike and Deb be flown to LA when "Margo's Cargo" finished its rapid climb to the top of the charts. They were given royal treatment for a couple of days with all the stars. Winston had matured well and was the most outgoing. Paul had long hair and earrings tattooed on his ear lobes. Walter hadn't changed a bit—still the longhaired dreamer with a honey-smooth voice and a range that bested Steve Miller. Davy had never made it out of the garage.

After the concert, the new drummer, Roger, met Mike and, in front of the band and MTV cameras said, "OK, Mike, I'm ready to get it over with."

"Get what over with?"

"Well . . . I'm the only one here you have not run through the ringer. Let's get it over with," he said strongly serious.

"Hmmm . . . it seems you guys have found your niche and your fame," Mike began. "I can't argue with a successful formula. And years of practicing law certainly haven't exercised any musicality I might have once had."

Roger looked utterly dejected. "Man . . . won't you even give me an opinion?"

"Well," Mike said a bit cautiously, "I only critique live rehearsal sessions, sorry."

The band, with MTV cameras catching all of their reactions, of course, overwhelmingly agreed. "Tomorrow night, usual time," Paul said laughing. Deb was amazed and tickled to be invited to a private jam session.

The cracks, pops and hums of bands tuning up sent more than a few tingles down Mike's spine. Years of legal training and family responsibilities slipped from his mind. He could almost smell the San Francisco sea as the band ripped into their powerful remake of a Led Zeppelin classic.

After a couple of songs were played, Winston said, "Mike, something's missing, isn't it?" And with that, the door opened and his brother Eric walked out with his wife. MTV had sent them plane tickets when they heard the story of days past, and a private cocktail party and concert ensued into the late night with many interesting guests stopping in to party.

The whole experience stirred a long-dormant passion in Mike. He was restless in the weeks following the trip. He quickly purchased a thundering entertainment system. Nights were spent on the couch—a sleeping Deb nuzzled next to him—watching intently as his favorite bands performed on the huge flat-screen TV.

Raging Currents soon cut a single for a Warner Bros. film. While Egg Productions' movie languished at the box office, the band's single, "Passionate Chords," astounded music critics and sold like hot cakes. "A deftly blended lyrical and rhythmic masterpiece," noted *Rolling Stone*.

The band renewed a more lucrative contract with Virgin Records, but not without insisting Mike be placed on the band's payroll. His title: Musical Consultant/Entertainment Attorney.

Thrilled with the opportunity, Mike quickly came up to speed on the legal issues of the industry.

Mike hoped his counsel would eventually lead to other business. He really made an impression on Virgin Records, his practice took off and he eventually succumbed and moved to Beverly Hills. That's a long way from Dog River, Toto.

No Conditional Waivers

Ronnie B. Williams grew up in South Mississippi. His father played high school football and raised Ronnie to be a ballplayer as well. Ronnie liked being with his father on the weekends mainly because his dad worked at the shipyard as a boilermaker foreman and was too tired to pay attention to the family when he got home on weekdays.

The high school coaches liked Ronnie. They saw him playing a linebacker or noseguard, since he was tall and big-boned for such a young man. Mr. Williams saw this as a waste; he felt his son could be a fine running back. He had visions that the college scouts would notice his son's speed and agility and the rest would be history.

After practice, Ronnie was too tired to answer his father's interrogations about the team. They began to grow apart. Weekends were spent with his football buddies and the girls who wanted to wear his letter jacket.

Work in the shipyard began to slow down and Mr. Williams had to lay off a lot of his workers. Some were longtime co-workers and friends. He felt bad about his friends, but he also feared his own layoff was imminent. The drinks after his shift began to get longer and stronger. Ronnie and his father began to fight with words, and though he wanted his father in his life, he didn't want a drunk he had to deal with every night. Mr. Williams began to say things Ronnie never imagined he would hear from his dad, and in the eyes of a drunk, their stressed relationship was Ronnie's fault.

One particular Tuesday, Mr. Williams showed up during football practice to observe. He had been drinking. Ronnie was at noseguard and Mr. Williams started slurring his shouts at Ronnie to "get with the program" and "be a real football player!" Ronnie was embarrassed, but his teammates respected him too much to say anything. In fact, they hurt for Ronnie as the shouts kept coming. That afternoon was a lifetime for any son to endure from the brutal inflictions of an impaired, sick parent.

The fight that took place between Ronnie and his father that night was one the family wishes to forget. Ronnie's mother stood by her husband. "The wife," as she was called, cringed at the sight of Ronnie pleading with her to help him help his father somehow. Mr. Williams' eyes were red with anger and from long bouts with the bottle. He approached his son aggressively. Ronnie stopped short of hitting his father, but not by much, and ran out of the house.

Ronnie was a star on the football team his senior year as a cornerback. Mr. Williams was too ill to see any of the games and died of alcohol-induced liver problems just before graduation. The entire football team attended the funeral, along with a tremendous number of his friends and fellow students he barely knew. Ronnie was strong and walked his grieving mother through the service. During the service, she turned to him and asked Ronnie to forgive her for what she had put him through. He just held his hand to her lips, signifying forgiveness wasn't an issue to him. He loved her no matter what.

The University of Mississippi recruited him with scholarships and Ronnie visited the coaches to accept. He had a surprise for them, though. He asked to be guaranteed a position as a running back. Of course, they wouldn't provide a guarantee to him for a position he had never played. That was ridiculous for him to expect. Thanking them for their time, he got up to leave and the head coach stopped him. "Why are you trying to force the University to guarantee you a position you've never played?" the coach asked. He proceeded to explain why that could not happen. Ronnie listened to their argument. He understood. Then they listened to him, something they had not done before.

The coaches realized football had taken on a new meaning for Ronnie. They were perplexed. Then, they made a mistake with Ronnie B. Williams. They played hardball. He was open to some compromise, but they offered none.

As Ronnie walked out of the gym, he felt proud. He wouldn't return. He met his mother in the parking lot as she waited to take her son back home. As he got into the car, his mother asked how it went. He told her there wasn't an agreement. The silence was deafening.

When they got home, Ronnie put on his running shoes and began to jog the streets he'd grown up on and into neighborhoods he was less familiar with as well. He kept running into the darkness of the early evening. Once back home, his mother put his supper out and they talked.

The next week, he had offers from some great schools to play ball. But none of the major universities were interested. Decision time neared.

The phone rang. It was his high school coach. Coach Bone wanted him to come down to the school. He asked Ronnie to dress out. He timed Ronnie with full pads and was surprised at his speed. Ronnie appreciated his help and willingness to approach the universities once more.

The University of Arkansas took a chance on Ronnie at Coach Bone's insistence, a decision they would relish. During his time with the Razorbacks, he showed great promise as a running back early on. It was in his junior year that he broke the rushing record for the most yards in a season when they realized he was one of the best running backs in the country. His dedication to practice was intense as he started his senior year, and it paid off with strong offers from pro football leagues after a great season. He decided, however, to become a free agent. Football would be secondary to dental school.

The first year without football confused him, as did the demands of school. He didn't miss the game as much as he thought he would, but he kept working out as if he were still in training. His speed increased, as did his agility. He figured the lack of bruised tissue made a difference.

Thanksgiving holiday, he joined his mother for her family's get-together. The first thing he noticed was that the house was in need of serious repairs, and Ron worried about his mother's finances. At Sunday services, Ron prayed things would work out for her.

The phone rang in his apartment the following week. Ron was being recruited to suit up for the Cowboys. Injuries had two of their running backs out and one more injury could leave them short. He was flattered, but wouldn't consider leaving dental school . . . that is until he was offered $70,000 per game, play or not. School would wait. Ron dedicated his first game to his father, and got to play enough to impress the fans and become their new idol. He was an overnight celebrity with TV anchors doing their best to make this a newsworthy event. With Ron, they had stellar material to work with, especially when they showed pictures of painters working on his mother's house a few weeks later.

He returned to school after two years, but in pursuit of a different career. Graduating with a business degree, his mother and fiancée by his side, he announced his candidacy for the senate seat vacated when the Democratic Senator from Mississippi resigned due to a cotton trading scandal.

Sometimes, they say, life goes full circle. Ronnie Williams did win that senate seat. He also went on to accomplish a lot of things. The greater his accomplishments, the closer he realized he was to his father.

Ron Jr. broke the news to his father, one spring evening at supper, that he wouldn't be training during the summer with the football team. He wanted to try out for swimming and gymnastics for his senior year. His goal was to be an Olympic swimmer. However, he would become a major university cheerleader if gymnastics prevailed over his swimming abilities. Whatever a father first thinks after hearing the news his son wants to be a cheerleader must be universal. But Ron Sr. didn't even break stride that night. He just looked over to his wife and shrugged his shoulders. Then he said "Go for it, son, now pass me the cornbread."

Herd South for Winter

Joel Sinclair had been out on the prairies for four years, moving cattle from place to place. His reputation among the cowboys was full of respect, and he was offered his own herd to deliver to the fertile grazing grounds of New Mexico. The size of this herd was exceptionally large and he had plenty of help waiting for him to give them a nod as part of the shapeup. His first herd of cattle driven southward was delivered ahead of time, which meant a nice bonus for the men. Inside the saloon he met his old friend, Darien, from his childhood. He was drinking quite heavily. Darien Post and Joel grew up in the Rockies near Augusta, Montana, and had been close friends—close enough that Joel knew Darien changed somewhere along the way. Their conversations were less enjoyable, and Joel could sense a hint of jealousy creeping into what had been a fairly tight friendship. He stayed tied to home so long before adventuring out into the country to search for his own life, having stayed at home with his mother, eating her cooking and learning to drink whiskey. Joel could well remember those times when Darien drank too much. It wasn't a pretty scene to witness.

"Joel! Joel!" Darien shouted as Joel walked to the bar. "Hello, D," Joel said calling him by his usual nickname. "What brings you here?" Darien asked. "I was just going to ask you the same thing!" Joel said. "Hell, I'm looking for some ladies," Darien said. "Well, any luck?" Joel asked. Another man laughed and shouted, "Him? Women?" The man offered a toothless grin and cackled with his drunken gang.

Joel put his arm around Darien's neck and they bellied up to the bar. Several men came in and patted Joel on the shoulder. "Good job, Boss. Enjoyed workin' for you," one said.

"Shit, Joel. Was that you bringing the herd in today?" Darien asked. "Yes, it was my first. Rancher in Wyoming got in a bind and gave me a chance. Up till now I was only a hired hand," Joel said. "Well, next time, get word to me and we'll be partners," Darien said holding his whiskey glass out to the bartender for a refill. "Let me buy this man one, too," Darien said. "No, Darien, let me buy. I just got paid, you know!" Joel said.

As the men drank generously over those blurred hours, their personalities flew in opposite directions. Darien adopted a hostile look, as he got drunker and drunker.

"Darien, you've had enough, dammit. Why is it that you can't fuckin' drink?" Joel said, getting pissed at his friend's ever-increasing rowdiness. As his last, taut nerve snapped in two, Darien threw his glass at the wall and growled, "You fucking high horse mother fucker! Can't tell me what to do."

Noticing the uproar, some of Joel's hired hands stood up. He waved them back down. "Darien, what is it with you? You can't hold your goddamn whiskey, you just shouldn't drink in the first place," Joel said, unconsciously turning up his sleeves. He too was a bit high. Blind with rage, Darien grabbed a bottle from the bar and hurled it toward a table of poker players. "Don't fuck with me, assholes," Darien seethed.

And the sick feeling in his stomach told Joel that the worst of the liquor had taken over. This was now a Darien unlike any he'd seen. He'd seen Darien in an occasional fight or some heated argument, but this was out of control. A man he had never known standing next to him with hate blaring from his eyes, his ears closed shut so as not to hear Joel's warnings to settle down.

One of the men at the poker table was furious. Joel watched him stand and take the aggressive ready-to-draw stance of a gunfighter. As he stood, waiting for Darien to make a move for his gun, Joel began screaming louder at Darien to turn around and let things be. Still unheard, Darien focused glazed eyes at the man, as other men scrambled for cover sensing a gunfight was inevitable. Joel jumped in front of

Darien, yelling at him to settle down. But, looking into eyes he didn't even recognize, Joel saw something terrifying. Darien looked back coldly, threw his fist effortlessly into Joel's stomach and pushed him to the ground. Before he could look up, Joel was deafened by the crack of a gun and crushed by Darien's body. Blood gushed over both figures, which lay still on the shabby floor.

Joel blinked, scrambled from under Darien with a terrified look and, scooping to catch his breath, forced out the words "Get the doctor, boys!" They rushed out into the street just as the sheriff sauntered casually in.

"Darien—don't die, Darien," Joel cried. Darien opened his eyes and looked at Joel. He tried to speak, but couldn't. Joel stared back into his friend's eyes while he died. Joel squeezed him close, as his bloody body lay lifeless on the floor of the saloon. A lifetime of friendship was dead after a few hours of reminiscing. Joel felt he was to blame, he should never have allowed Darien to take his intoxication to the level of hell.

Tears poured from Joel's face as he searched for thought about what had happened, thinking about Darien's wonderful mother. How could he ever bear to tell her the truth? The sheriff's mouth moved endlessly, but Joel's ears had closed and he heard nothing. The sheriff finally asked some of Joel's hands to take him to the hotel.

"Boss, come on, Boss," Justin pleaded. Joel's top rider, who had met him in Colorado two years earlier, finally barked at his incoherent boss, "Joel Sinclair, get up!" Justin forced Joel away from Darien's body. "I'll take him to the room," Justin said to the sheriff as they stumbled out of the saloon.

"Justin, oh shit, Justin. What's happened?" Joel asked, resting his head on Justin's shoulder. "Boss, you have had a lot to drink. Let's get some sleep and we'll talk in the morning."

They walked upstairs—a gallery of people stared. Once in his room, Justin took off Joel's boots and wet a towel to wash the blood off of his face. "No, dammit. Leave me alone," Joel said holding his head between his bloody hands. "Leave me alone, Justin." As Justin walked out, he looked back at Joel crying on the floor by his bed.

"Walter, find out who the son of a bitch was who did the shooting," Justin said to one of the hands as he walked over to the sheriff.

"Sheriff, that man shot a drunk. It wasn't no gunfight," Justin said. The Sheriff responded in an imperious tone, "Now son, you're a fine young man. We've had enough trouble here for one night. I'm asking you to take your men and go to bed." "Yes, sir. But I saw what happened here. It ain't right," Justin said.

The next morning, as the sun rose and the town began to awaken, Joel opened his eyes and stared at the ceiling. As reality set in, he cleaned up and went downstairs. Justin was waiting in the lobby.

"Mornin', Boss" he said as Joel acknowledged him. "May I join you for some coffee?"

"Yes, Justin, please do," Joel said quietly.

Justin sat stiffly as Joel stared into the kitchen. Justin wasn't sure what to say. He decided to wait until Joel spoke. The server brought coffee and cinnamon bread. Joel took no notice.

"Justin, I need some answers about last night. Let me make myself clear—I *need* answers. The best you can tell. If you ain't too sure, then don't do no guessin'."

"Boss . . . ," Justin began, and pulled his chair in close to the table. He moved everything on the table to the side and leaned forward to whisper. Joel moved in close, too. "Darien is dead. He's been around town over a year. Not many friends, but was one of the best horsemen and blacksmiths around. He made good money breakin' horses and helpin' at the stable. He's been in a couple of fights, but nothing serious. Bartender says he got drunk regular, but never paid no 'tention to nobody. Usually not a mean man of the whiskey."

Joel sipped some coffee and leaned forward. "What'd he do to piss off that man?" he asked. "All I can get is that he threw a bottle at them, but there's somethin' else." "You're right, boss, there is." Justin replied. "Like what?" Joel now had his keen sense of listening turned way up.

"Like, that man is very rich. We found out he has a lot of money in the bank here and has been buyin' up some land on the river. One farmer got drunk here and said he'd never sell his place to him no matter . . . well, he got shot down too."

"Who is this fella?"

"William Anderson, from Boston."

"What's he doin' here?"

"Won some land in a poker game and decided to stick around. Only other word I got is that the sheriff lives in a house he owns."

Joel pushed his long hair back from his face and stared into his coffee. He sensed something foul, but it looked hard to prove when the people stacked up against them held the facts.

"I'll need a wagon to bury Darien in the mountains nearby."

"Already have one ready, Boss. I'll go with you."

"No. You're in charge of seeing the men off and getting back to Wyoming to find us some more work. I'll meet you in three weeks," Joel said as he stood up.

"Oh, one other thing," Justin said as they walked onto the porch. "Those cattle we delivered went to a farmer who owes a lot of money. Mr. Franklin, right?"

"Yeah, Franklin's his name," Joel said.

"Well, if we hadn't got that herd here, he wouldn't have been able to pay his note. He's gettin' nice pay to let the cattle graze here over the winter."

"Who has the note?"

Justin shrugged his shoulders indicating he wasn't sure, but they both guessed Anderson probably had it. At least, Anderson hoped he could've been in a position to take it when Franklin defaulted to whoever had the paper on that farm.

"Justin, find out any other farmers around here who need a herd to tend to this winter. We'll help them out if we can. Also, find out who's sendin' cattle to Anderson. Send me a wire in Augusta."

"Have a good trip, Boss."

"Justin, you shouldn't call me Boss when we're together."

"Yes, sir!" They slapped each other on the back and walked to the stable.

"Mistuh, you takin' Darien home?" a black man asked from inside the stable.

"Uh-huh," Joel responded.

"Well, I'm proud to knows ya, suh. Mistuh Darien was a fine man. Gonna miss him 'round here," he said.

"He was a fine man," another voice said and, as Joel turned, he could see the blacksmith approaching.

"I'm John Arnold, the blacksmith," he said.

"Hey. I'm Joel Sinclair."

"Darien was the best help I've ever had," John explained. "He didn't want me to pay him in wages much. He'd just get drunk and lose 'em. He was building a carriage for his mother with his wages. It's over there," he said pointing to a beautiful red buggy.

Joel walked over and admired the meticulously crafted piece, truly one of the finest he'd ever seen. The black man took a cloth and began dusting it while talking quietly to himself.

"It needs just a bit more work," the blacksmith said, breaking the silence. "Luther and I'll fix it up. Next time you're here, you can pick it up and deliver it to his mother. Meanwhile, take that wagon over there. We've packed all of his belongings, too. That's the least Luther and I can do to see he gets a good burial. Luther, go get a team and show this gentleman to the undertaker's shed," John said while shaking hands with Joel.

Meeting Darien's friends at the blacksmith's shop brought a small smile to Joel's face. He knew Darien had been able to make a life after all.

The undertaker loaded the wooden coffin onto the wagon. Joel tried to pay him, but he refused. "Where's the preacher?" Joel asked. The undertaker looked up and glanced into Joel's eyes. He pointed to the end of the street. "You'll find Preacher Thad down there," he said as Joel spurred the team of horses with a few yanks of the reins.

Joel's deep voice commanded the team of horses and the wagon stopped next to the preacher's house. A man walked out. His piercing eyes fixed on the wagon.

"Darien was a good Christian," Joel said as he felt the preacher's hesitation. "I thought you could bless his body or something."

The preacher stepped slowly off the porch and Joel jumped off the wagon. "You a friend?" the preacher asked. "Yes, we're old friends from Montana, town called Augusta."

"Any family left there?" he asked. Looking up, Joel responded, "Well, uh, Darien's mother lives there, and his . . ." "No, I mean you," the preacher interrupted.

"Yeah, my parents and sister," Joel said, a bit surprised and nervous his devotion to Christianity might be quizzed.

Preacher Thad stared at Joel, then at the wagon, and then back at Joel. "Let us pray," he said abruptly. He took Joel's hand and held it beside the coffin.

"God, a tragic death is sad without the knowledge of your Kingdom. May Darien's death give us strength to live with your word. Bless his friend who takes him home. Give him courage to confront Darien's family with truth. Help us all to forgive, even the man who takes the life of another."

Joel opened his eyes. He wiped them since he'd felt a slight bit of wetness on his lids, looked to the preacher and said, "Thank you, sir."

Again, the preacher fixed his gaze on Joel. "Son, Darien came to church fairly regular. A fine addition to our congregation. I prayed over his body this mornin' early. I've asked the Lord to accept him into Heaven. I pray for you now, and for our own souls, as we reason with this senseless death. Go on now, but promise me you'll send word of his family to me."

Joel nodded as the two shook hands. He climbed back on the wagon. Preacher Thad stood and watched as Joel moved slowly north. Joel looked back until dust spinning from the wheels obscured the preacher's figure.

The ride was bumpy and, after three hours, it was time to set up camp. Joel wasn't hungry. Instead, he chose to drink with his dead friend. Before the fire was reduced to quiet coals, Joel's soft, slurred words to Darien mixed with the night air.

Once in the mountains, the cool air helped keep the body from decaying too fast. Joel wanted to bury Darien on the side of Indian Mountain where, as children, they'd hunted one particular trophy elk for several years. But that spot was another three days' journey without too much trouble from snowstorms in the mountains. He decided to bury him at the end of one more day of travel.

Joel began looking in the mid-afternoon and saw a beautiful open space where he figured the ground might be soft enough to dig into. As he set up camp and wondered of the exact spot to bury his friend, he heard the bugling of an old elk. He listened as the beautiful animal made its famous strange sounds, which were well echoed by the landscape. Memory and imagination flurried. The evocative sounds continued as the sun disappeared over the mountain peak. He would sit and listen until the darkness provided the stars with their stage. He would eat a rabbit he'd obtained earlier in the day for dinner, and the burial would be in the morning.

The morning's early lighting was in full strut when Joel was awakened by noises from that old elk. He instinctively grabbed his rifle and went for a look. Across the valley, he could see the magnificent creature with its head extended out into the morning air. It was a trophy. Suddenly, Joel knew where to bury Darien. Emotion, which would have to wait, and his dirty hair were accented by smiling lips as he headed for the wagon, thinking what a beautiful day it was to put his friend to rest.

As he dug on the spot where the elk had bugled minutes before, he began to get hot. The sun and rocky soil made him sweat and furrow his brow. He worked at it without rest and, each time his arms became tired, the thought of the man shooting Darien gave him new strength.

Pulling the wagon alongside the hole in the ground, Joel pulled one end of the coffin until it fell softly to the edge of the grave. He walked to the horses and pulled them forward. After an eternity of dragging and scraping sounds, he heard the coffin fall into the earth accompanied by a quick rush of escaping air from the rude grave.

Dirt and rocks dropped with hollow sounds on the coffin. When it was covered, Joel lined rocks on the top of the pile of dirt. "Darien, with all my love. I'm going to miss you." Joel bid his friend a long goodbye and said a prayer.

The hills around Augusta were memorable as he approached days later. The scenery varied a lot with the seasons. It was cool as Joel headed up to Darien's mother's place. He'd been riding seven days with nothing to do but think. Panic lingered. He had no idea what to say. As he saw the fence around the plain white house, all previous thoughts vanished. All he could see were the winter flowers in the yard. What he heard was Preacher Thad talking about truth.

He stopped and looked from the wagon. Mrs. Post was obviously cooking, judging from the smoke coming from the kitchen flute. He could imagine the smell the stove's goodies were filling the house with.

Tucking in his shirt, he went over to the well to wash his face. The cool well water smeared the dust as he felt his pockets for his bandana to wipe off the dirt. When he heard the door of the house open, his heart began beating rapidly. She stood looking at him. Her curiosity waned a bit when she recognized Joel. Her gray hair blew across her face. Joel moved up to the porch. "Hello, Joel," she said in a tone wishful of this being a courtesy visit, "Why, this is the most exciting time I've . . . " Joel hung his head low, as she stopped her welcoming ritual.

"Mrs. Post," he said with a nod.

"It's Darien," she said, appearing to be unsteady on her feet momentarily.

"Yes, ma'am."

"Sit down Joel and tell me. Is he all right?"

Joel sat down and felt numb. He surveyed the yard and porch with his eyes, then looked at her. The words started coming out, but he couldn't hear himself speaking.

"He was killed two Tuesdays ago. I was there. He died right away—a gunshot." She looked at him, strongly, almost as if she already knew.

"I took a job movin' cattle and we met in the saloon. I didn't expect to see him. He got real drunk. So did I. We were happy to be together. He disturbed a poker game and some man shot him when he moved toward his gun."

"He pulled out his gun?" she asked.

"Well, not exactly. He moved at it. He wasn't going to pull it, I'm sure," Joel said, feeling like he was being cross-examined.

"And you were there?" she asked.

"He hit me and I fell to the floor. The gunshot deafened me and he fell. I'm so sorry, Mrs. Post."

"He was a good boy. The liquor was bad to him. I knew he might die. I loved him, but I was always afraid he would die a young man. He never found a wife. That might have helped."

She started to cry. Joel sat quiet holding her across her dainty shoulders while he was looking around the house at familiar objects. He could remember Darien walking in the house always giving his mother a kiss.

"It's going to be hard for me but, Joel, please tell me the whole story," she said. And Joel began from the beginning. She listened carefully to every detail, to every curious unexplained detail.

"You buried him?" she commented. "That's so nice. You must take me there, and to visit his home."

"I will. It's late in the year now. How about next July when it's not too muddy?" he asked.

"That'll be nice."

"I brought you his belongings, but there is something left there for you. It'll be waiting for us in summer.

"Can you take me up to the church now?" she asked.

"Sure."

And they rode to the church. She headed inside and Joel walked next door to inform the preacher of the sad news.

"Son, we worry often about you. Won't you stay here?" the father asked. "Well, for now it looks like I'll be busy moving cattle," said Joel, "that is, until I can find out more about the man who shot D."

Joel stayed two days before trading his wagon and team for a fine mare and heading into the quiet town of Augusta to see if he had a wire from Justin.

"Hey young man, how's ya bin?" Mr. Avery inquired from the telegraph office.

"Just fine, Mr. Avery, how are you and the family?"

"Ever botie good. Have sometin' fer ya."

He handed the envelope to Joel and Joel handed him a handsome tip. He started to refuse it when Joel stopped him and said he wanted him to have it.

He opened the envelope. It read:

JUSTIN TO JOEL. SIR. ANDERSON DOIN BUSNES W/CATTLE RNCH IN E. MNTANA NAME OF BEAR LAKE. MR. VAUGHT. REGARDS.

Joel would ride to Grand Rapids and take the stagecoach to the eastern part of Montana. The trip took about a week due to poor weather. He arrived and checked into the local hotel. After dinner, he went to the saloon to gather information from the bartender.

He bought a horse from the stable and rode north to a town called Hope, where Bear Lake Ranch was located. Just outside town, he saw a sign to the ranch. Having some daylight, he decided to stop in.

"I'm here to see Mr. Vaught," Joel said to one of the hands.

"Who's a-callin'?" he asked. "And why you a-callin?"

"Joel Sinclair. Need to speak to him about his cattle business."

The man shook his head and laughed. "Look, kid, why don't you go on aback to where'ere you came," and started walking away.

Joel whipped his horse and galloped past him up to the house. He heard the hand pull his pistol and cock it. He stopped and looked at him. "I ain't going nowhere till I speak to Mr. Vaught first. I'm not looking for trouble." Mr. Vaught walked out on the porch. He was a big man with a firm belly hanging in front of him. He motioned for the hand to put down his gun.

"What can I do for you, son?" he asked.

"You can let me move some of your cattle south for the winter, and back in summer. I just delivered 1,400 head to Mr. Franklin in Green Valley Holler. I heard you had cattle nearby."

"Franklin? He took 1,400 head?"

"Yes, sir."

"Come in, we'll talk. Blake, take his horse to the stable, please."

As they walked inside, his wife looked from the kitchen. "Will you stay for supper?"

"He's stayin' for breakfast too, Martha," Mr. Vaught said. "Go freshen up and we'll talk at supper."

Joel could tell that something about Franklin caught Vaught's curiosity. At supper, Vaught asked all about Joel's personal life, family and ambitions. After eating, they retired to the living area for a glass of whiskey and a smoke in front of the fire.

"So, tell me how you came to know Mr. Franklin," he said.

"Well, frankly, I don't know him. I was working in Colorado and, just outside of Ft. Collins, I heard someone was needed to move cattle south. I applied and got the job because some of my fellow hands wanted to work with me. A Mr. Freedman there put the herd together. He knew of Mr. Franklin."

"That's interesting. How long did it take?"

"Twenty-one days."

"That's fantastic, Joel."

"Thank you, I was happy with the way it went."

A couple more drinks and some stories passed. Vaught looked at Joel a moment, then moved closer to the fire.

"Joel, what brings you out here really?"

"What do you mean?"

"Son, you must know most of my cattle are in New Mexico already. Besides, I have quite a network of people."

"Then why'd you invite me in?" Joel asked bluntly.

Vaught paused and smiled. "You know, I kind of like you. But aside from that, something is on your mind. You can talk about it or not."

Joel sat quiet a moment. "It goes something like this," Joel started, standing up and lighting a cigar.

"I rode into Green Valley with my first herd. Unexpectedly, I run into an old friend and I have drinks with him in the saloon. We drink a lot and he gets terribly drunk and throws a bottle of whiskey into a poker game where a Mr. Anderson sits. Anderson's fuming—not just at that—I figure he's mad 'bout the fact I got that herd to Mr. Franklin in time for him to make his note on the farm. Anderson stands up. Old friend drunk Darien taps on his gun and Anderson shot him dead, right there, and about as fast as this story is to tell. I hear you're doing business with this man Anderson and I'm here to do something. I haven't quite figured just what that is yet."

Vaught put down his drink and walked to the window and stared into the darkness. He then sat down and looked at the fire a moment.

"That's the story?" he asked.

"Yes, sir, that's about the way it goes."

He slugged down his whiskey and looked at young Joel. "Go up and get some rest. We'll talk in the morning."

The next morning, Martha cooked a hearty breakfast. Joel finished and thanked her graciously. "Mr. Vaught, I'm sorry if I have been an unwanted guest. I feel better having told you this personally."

"Thank you for coming, son. I have asked Blake to ride with you back to Grand Rapids. He'll need to tend to some business there for me. Let me give you some advice, which I hope you'll heed. Jealousy and hate are two ingredients to failure. Don't ever make decisions or judgments when they are present."

"You're right, sir. The preacher prayed that we forgive a man who harms another. I have a hard time forgiving, but I know he's right, too."

"You're smart to remember what the preacher tells you," Martha said having overheard them. "I've packed some food for your trip. Please come back and see us again," she said, giving Joel a kiss.

"Thank you, ma'am," he said.

By the time Blake and Joel reached Grand Rapids they were best friends. They went to the saloon to drink and play poker. The next morning Joel found Blake had already gone, so he went for breakfast alone.

Joel stayed in Grand Rapids calling on ranchers and girls. He met a beautiful girl, Sheryl, and stayed for an extra week. The ride back to Augusta was cold as winter was settling in. As he rode through town, Mr. Avery hollered, "Joel, you got a message yesterdee!"

Joel opened the telegraph. It read:

JOEL SINCLAIR FROM JOHN ARNOLD, BLACKSMITH. MR. ANDESON KILLED IN PKR GAME LAST NIGHT BY A FRIEND. NAME BLAKE. NO ARREST EXPTD. LUTHR SNDS REGARDS TOO. RED BUGGY READY.

Joel stood silent. He then rode to visit Mrs. Post. He laid the note down. She read it and looked up to Joel in an endless silence. Forcing a smile, she said, "I've always wanted a red buggy."

Mad Drag Queen

Maybe the mothers deserve the right to gain sympathy for their murdered. They don't display any sentiment on the promenade. They act content, and slightly a bit into the fame surrounding their marches each Thursday at three in the afternoon on the Plaza de Mayo, in the beautiful city of Buenos Aires.

Oh yes, it's extremely sad to have a loved one leave home one morning for work, then never see or hear from them ever again. Like most unreal stories, there are different versions and varying theories of what happened. One thing seems clear—these missing men aren't coming home. The pigeons are en masse in the plaza. They eat corn from the hands of people, mostly children. They are revered somewhat. The Pink Palace is for real, though it would make a nice title for some off-Broadway play about a gay dictator who nellied up the royal digs. It really is pink, even without Broadway.

The taxis don't blow their horns much, and that's so cool! They don't have stop signs or traffic lights at a lot of intersections. It seems to work fine. Makes you wonder why we have such a problem getting invited into oncoming traffic elsewhere, when here they just expect you to join in.

While you visit, you most likely won't get invited to a dinner party with lots of Argentine wines poured into Waterford and beef cooked 16 different ways. But you won't starve fending for yourself on the streets with a restaurant scene as vibrant as the one here. You can vaguely imagine that one of the embassies has a guest list with your name on it!

Pretty people. Some eye contact. The crazies. Lots of vendors. Not much new to shop for. More eye contact. That beautiful street. Those cool people. Great attitude control. Street names that are pleasing to hear and they're not too complicated to navigate on your own.

So young with energy and yet so poised with the influence of times past, don't cry for me Buenos Aires. When a place touches you like this, the experience lustfully scars you in ways you will find impossible to shake off—much like dealing with a mad drag queen. No way that ends with ease, and neither will the impact of this amazing place. It will persevere and, as you tolerate the man in drag, you will overlook the imperfections and come back here again.

How'd I get the same lady to sit next to on the airplane the second leg of the trip home as the first? She's well in touch with the Almighty, it seems. There's something to this, but the bad breath is enough to keep me guessing. Lord, give her a Breathsaver, and soon.

The critic in me says the steak is too tough to chew, however, it is full of flavor. That's not all, kids. They don't bother with vegetables in this city of zillions of people (of all the heritages you can imagine). A heaven of sorts for those of you with parents who tell you to eat all of your broccoli before you leave the table.

The four or more floors of the disco are unreal. They make you feel important just being there. The people have almost no (I mean none, not any, nada) attitude.

Go to the cemetery? What kind of guy do you think I am? But, when in Buenos Aires, you do go there and wonder just what those various things in among the coffins scattered with dead flowers and unlit candles are doing? Eeek.

(The music is blaring in my headset on DL 104, Sao Paulo to Atlanta, and the fucking overhead light keeps going off and on. I'm sure people would just love to see me quit writing and turn the son of a bitch off. But, I've a tad bit more to remember.)

The architecture shows off early romantic sensibility and sophistication. The pollution tells a different story. The trip over to Colonia, Uruguay, is like running over to Petit Buoy Island from Tall's Marina at Dauphin Island—or Washington to Baltimore, San Francisco to Napa,

Key West to the Tortugas, NYC to the Hamptons—some equally interesting short trips full of anticipation.

The bicycle ride in Uruguay was safe in every way imaginable. Much more so than in Atlanta. Speaking of which, some guy wearing an Auburn University cap at the disco doesn't understand my Spanish (few people do), but when English flows it is revealed his home is only one block from my home in midtown Atlanta. Like the song . . . it's a small world after all, it's a . . . stop that!

The lady next to me again on the plane says, "Hang on, Jesus is on the way again soon," but until then we'll just have to deal with life's misfortune and suffering a bit longer, I guess she means. Much of this city is impoverished, something you probably won't see when you visit here. And like those mad drag queens, you'll deal with it if you must.

Whoa, Nellie

"Freedom of speech and the rights that go with the First Amendment are, not by accident, at the top of our constitutional rights," Abigail Nell Williams taught her sixth grade class at Leinkauf Elementary. "This means that when our country was being established, being able to express your feelings without fear someone might hurt you was very important. They wanted us to be able to say what we felt like saying, except of course that it should be decent and proper. What we might call moral."

As she spoke, the aging teacher-of-35-years' mind wandered. She recalled some of the tests and events in recent history where freedom of expression prevailed, even though not popularly accepted.

"My day was just fine," Nellie said in reply to a polite inquiry from her friend Marnie Talley. "I always enjoy class when I get across a complicated issue for sixth graders—who often act like third graders—and somewhat think that most all of them understand me. Marnie, do you ever question the integrity of our Constitution, I mean, to think of the possible pitfalls of, say, our rights to free speech?"

"Well, I've never thought of possible pitfalls. Like what?"

"Like saying it's OK to preach communism."

"But no one listens to those sort of things, Nell."

"What if they did?"

"But, they won't. That's why we're all a basically decent society compared to those communists."

"Now, Marnie, let's just suppose some controversial topic came up. What if the news picked up coverage of the issues and some of us listened to the somewhat radical views and, just suppose, they made a wee bit of sense?"

"Like what? What can you possibly think of that could be like that? And don't even talk about Darwin to me," Marnie said as she poured iced tea. The two headed to the wicker chairs on the porch facing Washington Square.

"OK, like what that Dr. Martin Luther King is saying to the Negroes," said Nell.

"Now, Nell, you don't believe those people are like us. After all, look at their schools and yours. You can't expect they'd ever be allowed to attend school with our children without totally disrupting things."

"Why not?"

"Why not! C'mon. Just because they're different. Maybe they have the right to work and attend schools, but not . . . "

"Wait. Explain *different*."

"You know what I mean. They're . . . they're not as cultured. They don't understand the same morals we do. That's not their fault. It is their heritage. We shouldn't thrust our ways on them, nor they on us."

"Well, I s'pose you and I aren't going to debate what cultured is or isn't. But, let me ask if you personally think they can be considered equal to us."

"They can pay taxes like we do, if they'll work," Marnie said sarcastically. Realizing she'd sounded a bit more racist than she should have, she apologized by waving off Nell's certain objection.

"OK, Marnie, let's talk about something else. You sound ridiculous. I've gone round and round with this myself and decided I'm gonna look at things differently from now on."

"Miz Williams, what protects us from people who say bad things about us?" Emily Proctor asked. This caught Nell with a bit of surprise—had her students decided it was OK to say bad things about people?

"You can't say something that isn't true," retorted Nell, "And you just shouldn't say anything that isn't nice." The girl seemed to accept this answer.

School was out now, as the summertime heat set in. Nell Williams drove to her house at Mullet Point on Mobile Bay where she had spent her summers for the past 20 years. Her husband died during the invasion at Normandy and, having never remarried, she would host his and her relatives for a few weeks each year (separately, of course). It seemed to counter the peacefulness the eastern shore is known for, having a house full of company all the while. That and those jubilees you wake up for at any hour to scoop up some seafood on the beach. Sometimes they both tend to break the loneliness disguised as boredom. As she drove through Fairhope, she stopped at the Standard Oil station where Mr. Burns would service her car with fresh oil and filters. He was much cheaper than those high-dollar dealerships downtown and she trusted that if he replaced something it must be worn out.

"Where's Mr. Burns?" she asked the young attendant.

"He's been ill. I'm his grandson Ralph."

"Dear word, son. How is he?"

"He's stable now. He's had a stroke."

"Oh my Lord."

"Are you a friend?" Ralph asked.

"We were in school together quite a while ago."

"Are you Mrs. Williams?" he asked.

"Why yes, I am."

"He told me you'd be stopping by," Ralph said. "I have been looking for you. I'll take care of your car for you. I'll have you ready in a jiffy!" And he began to open the hood to check things out, under Nell's watchful eye.

"You live at Mullet Point, right?"

"Yes, I do."

"He showed us your place once, when we were going to Oyster Bay to get some shrimp for the freezer."

"Well, since you know where I am, I hope you'll stop by. Please promise me you'll stop by. I'm sure there will be some treats on the stove!"

"How can I resist that offer?" he said. "I'll just pull your car in to the lift to get the oil changed now."

An hour later, Nell was on her way and delighted to have spent time with such a fine young man. In that hour, she found out he was going to be a freshman at Fairhope High School in the fall. He had hoped to be able to attend summer football practice but, with his services needed at the station, that would not be possible. His father and mother both worked for the shipyard and he was their only child. In many ways he felt closer to his grandfather, but Nellie knew that was quite normal and told him so.

One afternoon, with the hot sun barricaded from getting to the ground by the combination of oak, pine and magnolia trees indigenous to the bay waterfront, Ralph drove up to her place. He had stopped at a vegetable stand and picked up a bushel of silver-queen corn. He and his grandfather would arrive with treats of their own. Mr. Burns couldn't get out of the pickup truck and was too confused to know exactly where he was. Nell patted him on the arm and he seemed to acknowledge her. Soon, he nodded off, and Ralph toted the corn to the house. "My word, Ralph, how can you expect I'll eat so much corn?"

"I bet you've 14 ways to cook corn, Miz Williams. Besides, with all the relatives and all you're expecting . . ." The cooled moving air under the canopy of trees would lull most anyone into a nap. As the time passed, the sun broke below the leaf line of the trees, and began to shine between the cumulus clouds. Mr. Burns' eyes began to squint as he awoke, getting his bearings. The mystery of his whereabouts dissipated from his facial expression with the setting sun across the bay so familiar to him, and he began to smile. He looked out, he continued to smile, he faintly groaned. He was undisputedly happy to be there.

"Can I bring him here again?" Ralph asked as he could tell it was very enjoyable for him.

"Anytime," Nellie answered. And as the summer progressed, Ralph and Nell became close friends, often sitting on the lawn chairs by the water with the truck parked close by so his granddad could watch and be watched. "My husband's brother is bringing his grandson next week for a few days, and he likes to fish."

Ralph's interest level shot up, "The specs are biting now! I can take them if they want, but we'll have to fish real early, before work. It's the best time, really!"

Ralph and Sonny fished every morning, and became great friends. It made Nellie so happy to have boys running in and out of the cottage and the refrigerator. It was one of her more memorable summers in several years.

Ralph called Nellie to break the news of his grandfather's death the week before Thanksgiving. She expressed her condolences and said she would be at the funeral. Nell sat with the family at Ralph's insistence.

The high school years were exciting for most Baldwin County teens, as life had really just not changed much over time. As the years transpired, Ralph attended college and later on law school, Nell remained a close friend and confidant. Being accepted for his first job, he called home to notify his parents. His next call was to Nell.

"Aunt Nellie," Ralph had come to call her.

"How are you, Ralph?"

"Well, I just got a job."

"Great days! When and where will you work?" Ralph spoke slowly so the retired schoolteacher could hear and make notes, as she had always done.

"I'm going to be a lawyer for a fine Boston firm!"

"Oh my gosh, and I don't s'pose you're fibbin' me either."

"No, ma'am. It was my top choice. I'm surprised they wanted me." Nellie started laughing, but Ralph could also hear what sounded like her crying, too. Law school had been tough for Ralph. He put pressure on himself to excel. Nellie had insisted he slow down, but he didn't. "I'll be coming home this summer and will see you over the bay," he said.

"No, Ralph, I'm too old to go over anymore." And Ralph argued the point until he realized her decision had been easy to make and was final.

They were in constant communication over her last years and Ralph's mother insisted he come visit her just before she died. The visit meant worlds to her and just watching her smile made all of the nurses know Ralph was quite special. The estate attorney called Ralph because she'd left some things for him, mostly old papers and pictures she thought he'd like to have. Ralph asked if they would ship them to him to his summer home in Nantucket. One Sunday afternoon, he opened the box and sorted through the papers, and began to look through the box when he came upon the following:

What you should know About our First Amendment
By Abigail Nell Williams

As he read, he could hear her voice speaking to him—accentuating certain words and softly saying some of the interesting points.

> *. . . for how do we ever learn if someone doesn't teach? It is perfectly sound for someone to say what he thinks, especially when he thinks differently than we, and why do we find that bothersome? Is it that we so often do not listen because we have our minds made up already? Or is there something else, much deeper than the lazy excuse of just thinking the same old way? And how painfully I know that the greatest danger to our future from the First Amendment is in not using it.*

The paper was magnificent. Ralph never knew she felt so strongly about freedom of speech issues, but could tell the underlying message was much more involved. He reminisced about some of the conversations when she had talked a lot of becoming an individual.

Due to this experience, Ralph's future would be affected. His career would be shaped by the teachings of a friend. Her voice surfaced and his view's would change. Locked in his mind, he now possessed the essence of Nellie's soul, written many years before her death.

> *To expect the individual to ever achieve independence from flawed teaching, where the possibilities are extraordinary and the mind will require excruciating flexibility to permit interpretations that certainly must arise over the course of time, herein exposes the potential vulnerability of our school system.*

In his time spent working with various causes, he focused on providing legal defenses to the challenges of higher education. Ralph Burns, Esquire, became one of the leading experts exposing faults of school systems across the country. His victories included school systems simply using out of date texts, to several ignoring the teachings of some of the greatest scholars, purposely choosing not to expose students to their teachings and opinions. He would end his argument with, "To quote the late Abigail Nell Williams, 'What good is freedom of speech when suppressed?'"

The Naked Girl Needs Help

The same underwear, no new deodorant and old earrings decorated the hungover, middle-aged divorcee as she struggled to brush all the way back to her molars. She wondered where her eyeglasses were, as well as a cap for her hurting head. Bumping it on the rafter added undue pain as she climbed down from the small attic of her host's guest loft. A very vocal "shit" accompanied the incident. The barefoot woman climbed carefully down the steps. At the bottom, she realized she had no recollection of her obvious ascent up the quite vertical stairs the night before. The need for an immediate and complete accounting of what had happened came over her like bad news from a stockbroker.

Taking the offensive, she blazed into the kitchen as if fully aware of everything she was supposed to be and exuding, magically, the confidence of a bulldozer in a cornfield. She heard mumbling as the screen door shut with two slaps on the frame. The dog came up from the old and worn Oriental rug that covered part of the kitchen floor, heading toward a more peaceful place to plop. She turned directly toward the coffeepot, a habitual move. She really felt more like having an Alka-Seltzer. This ritual, however, helped her composure as she turned to see who might have congregated in front of the unlit fireplace (it was September and the coast of Georgia was still quite warm).

No newspaper had made its way into the house and one of the Jeeps was gone, suggesting Louise had gone to the beach for her morning swim. But, Louise was outside on the swing reading and, barefoot, she began looking for a safe place to land and get her bearings because the missing Jeep clued her in that there was more to remember.

"Good morning," she asserted to Ida, who was buried in her chair reading about olive oils from the Mediterranean.

"And good morning to you," Ida delivered her greeting without looking up from the book. Mixed signals being delivered in a tone difficult to interpret, she asked her first seemingly safe question.

"Is Janet up yet?" she asked Ida.

"Yes, they're all clamming," Ida said. Suddenly, the barefoot and hungover Lucille realized she had missed the clamming trip she had quite demandingly orchestrated the day before.

"Oh, shit."

"Yes, I was afraid you'd feel that way," Ida said.

Lucille then began her first line of defense by taking the offense, "Why the hell didn't they wake me up?"

Ida thought momentarily, then chose not to respond. But there was a quite evident reason. Lucille had taken drunk late into the night with a much younger guy visiting from down the beach. Ida left the beach early in the evening, when they were laughing at the idea of skinny-dipping. She figured, reasonably, that the hard-core revelers might end up in the nude, dipping in the surf under the beautiful moonlit night. But it just wasn't the scene for her. She had lots of sleep to catch up on from her hectic pace in New York City, and dealing with a bunch of drunks on the beach after clubbing with her all-night partyers at Club Roxy was just a bit too unsettling.

Young Troy, however, was not about to miss the opportunity and was playing the game with ease. He cooed over Lucille most of the night. She played the attention LA-cool and kept a fresh cocktail nearby. The ride on the beach found a bump and upset the cocktail, spilling it on her breasts and everyone began laughing as Troy removed his T-shirt to dry her off. Next, she was pouring the mostly vodka drink onto Troy's chest and dog-licking it off as everyone watched.

"Dammit, you're salty and sandy. I feel like I'm drinking a fucking margarita!"

By then, the last of the party was looking for a place to swim. As the Jeep stopped, David refilled Lucille's cocktail, at her insistence because she would never have spilled it if he "knew how to fucking drive." Her bossiness was well received, because she was worth the entertainment.

Music by the Pretenders was playing so loud that the distortion from a blown speaker shook the hood of the Jeep.

Troy dropped his suit and trotted bare-assed into the surf, which was moderate in intensity. His dive underneath a breaking wave took him farther into the deep. As he lay looking up into the sky full of objects, he heard Lucille yelling "Troy, don't leave me here, asshole." He could see the shape of a person being tossed around in the rough surf. He body-surfed up to her and pulled her out to where the waves were less severe. There, she tried to have Troy hold her close as their nude bodies brushed into each other in the ocean, but she was too heavy and drunk for Troy to oblige her wishes.

"Let's go back to the beach," he said.

"Not yet, I want to swim," she said with her eyes half-closed. But Troy knew she was past the point of being able to swim alone and he pulled her inshore.

David saw Troy struggling in the surf as he attempted to get her ashore. He excused himself from the others citing, "The naked girl needs help," (pronounced neck-ed) and he rushed to aid Troy in beaching Lucille.

"I'm fine, I'm fine," she kept saying. They tried to get her up on her feet to walk when a big wave knocked them all down. "God dammit, you're pissing me off," she said after rolling halfway up on the beach. The half moon reflected off of her skin as she struggled to get up on her own before falling backwards. Troy reached down and held her under her arms and David grabbed her legs as they managed to get her firmly up on the beach.

She tried one last stunt to show she was still in control of herself. After Troy pulled on her shorts, she reached for a cigarette. Lying down in the back of the Jeep, she passed out trying to light it.

David looked at Troy and said, "Pard-ner, you can take the Jeep home, but you've got to help me get her in her bed first."

Louise had been the first to bed the night before so she had heard most of the stories as the morning passed. She and Lucille were old friends and she gave her a poker stare as she walked by on the way to the kitchen.

"Love, we need to talk," Louise said as she passed. Barefoot Lucy stood in the kitchen while Louise gave her a combo of "shame on you" and "you need to apologize." She rubbed her necklace nervously, and approached her defense with appropriate caution saying, "I needed to blow it out. Hell, I'm glad to have friends to take care of me."

By the time the clam diggers returned with a big bucketful, they were in good, joking moods and the barefoot girl approached them with the look of submission from the wrestling ring.

Troy telephoned to check on things and Lucille grabbed the phone and said, "We were naked, honey, and I don't remember a thing. I'm not sure what that says about you!"

The afternoon progressed with warm breezes and moderate activities like backgammon and stacked-up dishes. The puppy dog lay near the A/C vent and Louise went for a massage. A car approached—Troy finally returning the Jeep. He brought fresh-cut daisies from the roadside and some blue crabs from a friend's trap. A bit later, an unexpected cooler-full of speckled trout caught on the pier arrived, delivered by the fisherman's son, Walt.

Wine began to accumulate on the bar as word of the clambake spread. A bottle of wine sort of satisfies the admission requirement to dinner on this special island.

Lucille spent countless hours in the kitchen, always close to a glass of "batch"—a concoction of herb tea and fruit juices, including prune juice, which is a modern-day hangover remedy designed in California by former flower children trying to enrich their abused bodies in-between yoga classes and psychic readings.

The boys returned from fishing and surfing, causing the usual reaction from the girls, who cleaned dishes and took out trash. They prepared a fire for the clams and a cooler for drinks. Any action like this usually calmed the women down, and it worked this time, too.

Saturday night, and the sky reminded them of the previous night. Toasts, dancing and flashbulbs filled the air with the smell of clamshells cooking on the grill. This incense instills a certain worth on the soul. And Lucille, too, danced alongside the others. They each made a quiet reflection to their island for providing them, once again, with a brain full of marshy memories.

Where the Desert Meets the Sea

A somewhat perplexed economy has grown out of a war with Bolivia. Those soldiers' bones that lie beneath the sand are buried in a warmth that has nothing to do with climate. A seaport so small, yet considered quite strategic. Mountains of rock, brown and tan dirt—a pale-yellow tinted landscape.

Westward is the ocean so magnificent. It is gray, blue, white and then all other colors mixed together. Birds fly above it, waves crash into the rocky shore, yet the splashed banks yield no vegetation.

The gunshots are silent. The strategy worked on the offensive and pride still prevails. Why don't we see more to this place than rocks and sand? You certainly feel it. The people show their pride and the economy barely hangs on with its shops selling radios and cameras.

After all, who can totally dislike a town that shuts down after lunch so everyone can go to the beach?

The border is near. Old Chevys and Fords carry families and friends across—the system is so confusing. Some hoods are up as the border police look for illegal items.

How can one think about returning to a place you really never meant to visit? The soul may be enriched if you don't go out of your way to miss places like this. If you look hard enough and keenly listen you just might discover beauty in its simplest and most natural form—just the way it was meant to be—like it most always has been.

Wait Listed

Lucious Kelly was walking down the street from his old family home. His parents were moving. They were in their 80s and needed something a little more manageable than a four-bedroom place with a large yard. Their children lived out of town now. Lucious came to take one last stroll.

Across the street, he noticed the top of a building through the trees and, though he slightly recognized it, he realized he'd never given it a second look. He walked around the block and there was this very small, yellow, brick and stucco apartment building tucked into the middle of the block. It seemed to have been there forever. The rooms were few, small and cozy. It was basically three stories, except for a couple of rooms on the fourth level creating a pointed structure much like a small-town city hall.

The corners of the building were rounded. Lucious stared and couldn't believe he had never paid attention to this sturdy structure before. He looked up through the open blinds and could tell the building was narrow because light shone through from the other side. No one appeared to be inside and he had a hard time telling how many apartments there were.

Ornate brickwork protruded from the tops of each end of the building, giving a balance to the architecture and forcing the building into the scenery surrounding it.

As he walked up closer, he realized part of the building was built on the property line. This caught his attention, as it was unusual. The first floor was elevated somewhat so that, up close, you looked up and only saw the ceiling inside.

This looked to be the perfect place for his parents to live, he thought to himself. His curiosity took him to the entrance, which had the number 617 next to it. A small foyer inside was empty except for some mailboxes and a wooden bench. The beautiful brick and granite inside was also built in a rounded style and every detail inside was solid and of very high quality. The light fixtures, for example, were iron and the door appointments were brass.

There were five mailboxes. One letter, to Ms. Adrian Stonewall, was sitting out on top of the counter next to the mailboxes. The address was 617 Shadowlawn, which surprised him. There was not a street called Shadowlawn anywhere near here.

Lucious couldn't find a phone number for leasing information so he walked outside. Looking upward—the building seemed so small the top floor apartment appeared magical—he had thoughts going through his mind telling him how perfect and simple a place this would even be for him and his wife to live one day.

Walking back to his parents' place, he kept looking back to see the beautiful brick structure through the trees.

"Mother, I've never noticed that apartment building on Davison Street."

"Oh, it's been there for years. That's the Shadowlawn building, some call it Oakshadow; most just call it the 617 Building."

"I can tell that it's pretty old. Who lives there? Did you ever consider looking into it for yourselves?"

"No. They tell me the waiting list has had some names on it for over 30 years. The last time an apartment came open was about six years ago. It's become a favorite subject for the magazines lately."

"I expect it's an elderly crowd."

"Yes. But you remember Mr. Griswald from school? He moved in there when I was in college. He's my age and still lives there."

"Who owns it?"

"Some widow, your father might know. Her grandfather built it."

At dinner that night Lucious asked his father about the landlord of the 617 Building. "That's Old Lady Stonewall."

"Does she live there?"

"No, she's still in that big house on Government Street."

On the flight home Sunday, Lucious couldn't get the apartment off of his mind. He decided he'd try to call Ms. Stonewall.

Wednesday morning, he called information and got the phone number for Adrien Stonewall on Government Street. He called her. The most pleasant woman answered and when he explained why he was calling, she proceeded to give him the information on 617. Her gentle description of the building was fresh and as if she had just opened it for tenants. There were five apartments, all two-bedroom units with wooden floors "that don't creak," one-and-a-half baths and a library "paneled with black cypress."

"Even though I've had names on the list for many years, most people move in when their name comes up," she said. Lucious understood. He wasn't sure why, but he understood.

"Any idea how long from now it might take me?"

"I'd expect about 15 years, possibly more."

"Go ahead, then, and add my name to your list."

Lucious died of cancer about 20 years later. His wife Isabelle took her time selling off most of the assets Lucious had acquired. She kept the house on Hilton Head Island, thinking she'd retire there someday when she closed down her bridal dress business.

Hilton Head gave her some nice years. Her friends included her in plenty of social functions and she enjoyed the island's ability to provide everything she needed. The past summer, though, was a hot one and she seemed to be tiring of the tourists unloading their golf clubs in front of the house, the restaurants always so crowded and the fact that her beach had become so congested. One day, something unusual happened. A letter, forwarded to her, arrived addressed to Lucious. She opened it and in it was a letter from the trust department of a bank in Mobile.

Dear Mr. Kelly,

We would like to inform you on behalf of the management that your name has reached the top of our list for an apartment in the 617 Building. We expect an apartment to be available for your inspection soon. Please contact us at your earliest convenience and convey to us your intentions.

Sincerely,

H.W. Smith, Trust Officer

There was an 800 number and Isabelle thought about calling to inquire. She knew it must be a mistake, but their letter appeared to be so legitimate that she was puzzled. She put the letter aside and forgot about it. A few days later, she was walking on the beach with her friend Mary Lou when the topic of investments arose. Isabelle mentioned getting the letter from the bank and her friend Mary Lou convinced her to call. "You never know, honey, Lucious might have inherited a fortune or something."

The next day she called the bank. Mr. Smith's secretary answered. "Mrs. Lucious Kelly?"

"Yes, that's right. I'm calling about . . . "

"Of course. You and Mr. Kelly got our letter. We've been expecting your call."

"Well, Mr. Kelly is deceased and I'm unclear about this letter."

"The 617 Building?"

"That doesn't mean a thing to me," Isabelle said.

"Mrs. Kelly, hold one minute. Let me get your file."

After a moment, a man answered. "Mrs. Kelly, this is Warren Smith. How are you?"

"I'm fine."

"Let's see now. It looks like your husband put his name on the 617 list in 1958, about 37 years ago."

"My word, we had been married almost 10 years. I can't imagine. What is this 617 Building?"

Mr. Smith began to explain the situation of how they became property managers after Ms. Stonewall died. He also explained to her that most tenants live there forever after moving in. And then, he explained the basic information about the apartments.

"Mrs. Kelly, Ms. Stonewall made some notes about her conversations with your husband. If you'd like I'd be happy to read them to you."

"Please do."

"She notes here that Mr. Kelly grew up down the street and was in town visiting his boyhood home and parents when he inquired. He is married with three children. His wife would love the place and he felt like they could retire there. Estimate of time—15 years. That's the length of time she estimated it might take before your name would expect to come up. She was off a bit, I'm afraid."

"Golly, Pete. I'm curious as a cat," she said.

"We'd love to show you the Adair apartment. It's lovely. Mrs. Adair died four months ago after living here for 18 years.

"I'm coming . . . I'll call my son and see if he'll drive me."

Her son thought she was a bit looney when she first called.

"C'mon, precious. Let's go to Mobile and see this. Your father had a clever sense about him. I want to go."

Her sweet, motherly voice excited him for several reasons. He, too, knew that she was approaching the age where decisions needed to be made, and he loved visiting his cousins there. It would be nice time spent with his mother and she always had something new to tell that he'd never heard before.

Curiosity spread throughout the family and even the friends in Hilton Head got into the act. When Lucious Jr. called his Mobile cousins to explain why they were coming, the excitement intensified. The 617 Building had become legendary in Mobile. It was considered an honor to reside there and it was a continual media favorite, as the magazines and so forth were always doing stories about the apartments and their tenants.

There was even a 617 historical society which met a couple of times a year. The list of prospective tenants is secretive. Once word got out you had a relative at the top of the list, you were an instant celebrity.

"Mr. Smith's office," the secretary answered.

"This is Isabelle Kelly."

"How are you, Mrs. Kelly?"

"Fine. I'm calling to make an appointment to come visit the apartment."

The drive down I-65 past exits like Pine Apple and Bay Minette brought stories of Lucious' early years. Lucious Jr. drove the LTD southward and listened. His father's friends had told similar stories after his funeral. His father really did have a good feel for which direction to turn in his life.

As they approached Mobile Bay from the top of Spanish Fort, Isabelle murmured in awe of the beauty. "Look at that, son. Isn't that something!" "Yes, Ma'am. I must admit it is." The Mobile delta extended to the causeway they looked down upon it from the hilltop view. The paper mill was pushing smoke skyward and the battleship *Alabama*, now at rest for the interested to see, was in the field of vision covered by a sky of clear air. The bait shops and honky-tonks on the way across the causeway gave fishermen and hunters places to congregate before and after their days of recreation. Coots swam in the water just next to the highway, not bothered by the cars speeding along. They approached the entrance to the Bankhead Tunnel, and Lucious Jr. secretly held his breath, just as he had done as a child once under the Mobile River.

They checked into the Admiral Semmes Hotel and there was a letter from Mr. Warren Smith. When they opened the door to the room, they found flowers and a bucket of fruit with homemade jellies from Sophia's Kitchen. A sure touch of Southern hospitality.

Mr. Smith gave instructions on how to get to his office in the morning, along with his home phone number, insisting she call to announce their safe arrival.

"Mr. Smith, this is Isabelle Kelly."

"Are you here safely?"

"Oh yes. We're fine."

"That's wonderful. Can I recommend a place for dinner?"

"Oh, we're probably just going to get something quick. Thanks anyway."

"Well, now, you call if I can help. Otherwise we will see you in the morning anytime you're ready."

"I expect it'll be around 9:00 A.M., is that OK?"

"Yes, Mrs. Kelly, that'll be just fine."

"Mom, let's drive by the 617 Building." Isabelle thought she'd say no to that request. As she thought about it, though, it did sound exciting.

They left their luggage unpacked and headed downstairs. The concierge knew exactly where they were going when he overheard Lucious Jr. mentioning Shadowlawn Lane.

The small, quaint building with its rounded edges and strong detail exuded a presence, almost fictional and fantasy-like. The eye followed its lines like an old yacht, with its stately existence commanding due respect with unquestionable fortitude.

Not much was said between them as they parked across the street. Several cars drove slowly by, their occupants looking the building over too. Lucious Jr. thought about his father's foresight. Isabelle wondered which apartment was hers.

The next morning began with coffee in the conference room of the Trust Department. Mr. Warren Smith and his secretary were delightful and were prepared for the many questions they had. Soon they walked into the 617 Building. Mr. Smith began to describe some of the features but not to the extent to unduly delay her seeing the apartment. She would move in a month later.

Once her life had downsized into a small, two-bedroom dwelling, Isabelle began to ghost write an article for the *Mobile Bay Magazine* once a month under the name Kelly Belle. Her view of Mobile gained a following from a tough audience of locals, as her views were refreshing reminders of why they all loved their hometown. Having the locals embrace her writing eventually caught the attention of some national publications and, before long, her column was syndicated. No one knew who she was, but all were convinced she had grown up there with plenty of sequins in her heritage.

She envisioned the bygone days in the current landscape of the old bricks and oaks. "The corner store smelled of licorice and her old friend Lucious could be seen escorting an older lady across Washington Square with a big blue hat which cooled her face from the hot summer sun," she once wrote, giving the only clue someone might have been able to catch. No one did.

Isabelle only left Mobile a few times before she died. Preferring visitors to visiting, Isabelle became nationally famous when she accepted an award for creative writing from the University of Mississippi at Oxford. Her writing over the years had been successfully published and, at the insistence of her children and grandchildren, she gave up her ghost status to receive the award. She accepted it in honor of her late husband. An excerpt from one of her articles was etched into the brass plaque screwed into the mahogany base holding the crystal bowl, " . . . Innocence . . . the rusting cypress hull of a Mobile Bay shrimper."

Life? Close, but No Cigar

"Ah ha!" he exclaimed when his oldest son, age 10, gave him a new tool for his birthday. "Just what I needed," he surely said. The flashbulbs popped and everyone sang. Cake, full of the exact number of candles, came out of the kitchen.

Head of his family and he's great at it. There were trips to the beach, the movies and the excursions out of state to see our country . . . for he's what we are to expect from dads.

Divorce? Child abuse? Insincerity? C'mon. We're talking about a provider. Food. Shelter. Love. Religion. That's this guy.

"UPP! There he is," he exclaims to the children as a fish begins to peel line from the reel. "Boy, this is great," a neighbor's son cries as he grinds away and sweat begins to drip from his face. "Ling! A good one, too. Keep reeling. I can just about . . ." He grunts as he sticks the gaff into the big fish. All the children laugh with big, wide-open eyes as the fish flops inside the boat. A real catch. Something that kid probably won't ever forget.

Nor will anyone forget that this man built that fishing boat himself in the garage.

"Thank ya, Jesus," the maid would say as she could hear his voice over the CB radio calling home to tell his family he was on his way. His wife would have dinner ready, and there would be coffee with dessert. Their peaceful time together. The children would finish homework and sleep.

Many things come to mind when thinking of him.

Perfect? "Close, but no cigar!" he would say.

He's soon to be elsewhere. In heaven, where his dreams become real. And his family will grieve because it shouldn't be. But, like his father and our fathers, it will happen. It should be known, though, that his hand reached out and touched many more than he'll know. His heart was his big smile and his lessons to us were in all the many little things he would do.

Interested? Oh, yes. But a surprise to him might be that he was interesting.

For in so many ways, he's bigger than life.

Worn Out

*Ruins of ancient object*s accepted for their place, easily. Details of the fabrication efforts outweigh the texture, which is like tradition—completely surrounding.

The local language echoes the alley. Time stands still, only we seem to age. Cobblestones under foot, enrichment lurks everywhere just a short walk.

Awaken late, the bookends of nightlife are worthy. The spirit people exude is a brilliant experience in and of itself. Be careful, it'll ruin you.

Pocket Full of Lira

Piazza Campo de Fiori in Rome is overseen by a statue of Bruno. Though I'm intrigued by his statue, I don't know much about him, or the people who walk up under his cloaked head to get a glimpse of his facial expression as they lay flowers at his feet.

Most days, the square is a thriving market for the farmers' produce. Common folks out buying greens and spices from the merchants give Bruno a buzz. Once they're gone, Bruno stays, watching out, protecting.

Joe J. Jenkins laid a flower at the base of the statue and moved on. JJ was in Rome for his first time and alone on his sabbatical from UCLA where he taught about the Renaissance. Divorced for three years, he was dating one of his former students who planned to join him in Florence for a romantic week. Meanwhile, he toured ruins, museums, churches and libraries to further his passion for history.

The small hostel near the Piazza Narvona was more expensive than he'd anticipated, but only by a meager number of lira. The location was ideal and the people were colorful and fun to be with.

"JJ, what did you have to eat for yourself all day?" Mrs. Torres asked as he walked in to get his key.

"I ate healthy today, Mrs. Torres. Ate fruit with Bruno."

Her eyes gleamed when she figured out that he had been to the piazza. "Si!" she began, "what do you think of about all those things going on over there?"

"Well, to tell the truth, I felt sort of out of place."

"Why you think that?"

"Oh, it is nothing. I'll go back for a café and fruit later and see if I can figure it out."

"Did you leave Saint Bruno the flower?"

"Yes, like you told me to."

"Molto bene."

Mrs. Torres had run the hostel ever since her father was killed in a knife fight with a drunk. Her two daughters helped her out and their husbands did most of the maintenance, when they were not busy restoring old furniture in their small shops in the alleys nearby.

Most mornings, coffee with milk was waiting when he ventured downstairs to the small dining area. But, this morning there was nothing and JJ headed out to splurge on a cappuccino. As he walked toward the coffee shop, he noticed a rain cloud and decided to turn back to the hostel for his umbrella.

His key wasn't where he'd just left it, and Antonio was nowhere to be seen. Antonio usually worked from midnight until 7:00 A.M. for Mrs. Torres and put the coffee on before he left. JJ didn't always see Antonio in the morning. The watchman often napped in the cloakroom before he left, in order to listen for the buzzer to announce a visitor, who he would then allow inside the gates.

JJ looked on the floor to see if his key had fallen down somewhere, then checked all of his pockets despite distinctly remembering leaving the key on the rack just minutes earlier.

He heard someone coming down the stairs and suddenly met eyes with a strange man who looked quite startled. JJ's Italian wasn't excellent, but he asked, "Who are you?" This broke the tension and the man charged him. JJ dodged him and pushed as he went by, causing the man to fall into the entry door and cut his head on the marble stoop. Blood immediately gushed from the gash as the intruder fled.

JJ didn't know what had happened and then it dawned on him that a robbery might have been happening. He ran out of the hostel and saw the man duck into an ally near the end of the street. He chased after him, afraid, then he heard a voice telling him to stop. He looked around, but there was no one. Then he remembered that Mrs. Torres' father had died while confronting a drunken robber. She'd warned him to leave any scene of terror.

"Antonio!" he said out loud as he ran back into the hostel, quickly punching the code to open the outer door. He'd entered it too clumsily and had to wait the ten seconds for it to recycle. Carefully, 4-2-4-2, and the click of correctness had him inside. He yelled for Antonio, but nothing. He ran upstairs to his room. It was locked. There was only one other guest in the 15-room hostel, and he ran up two flights to see if he was in. It was 6:45 A.M. "Signore, signore," he yelled, knocking on the very hard wood door.

He heard a voice inside saying something he couldn't understand, and ran back downstairs shouting for Antonio all the way down. The cloakroom, he thought. Sure enough, Antonio was there. His body lay slumped with his bloody head wedged into a position only a lifeless body could endure. Panicked people sometimes make good decisions. He picked up the telephone and dialed "0." The operator answered to hear him yelling, "Hostel Della Pace, urgent, urgent!" Finally, he heard the best words he'd ever heard: "I'll have the police there in five minutes," the operator said.

Holding Antonio, it looked as if he'd been beaten, with blood dried on his mouth. He was sure he heard him having difficulty breathing when the other guest, Mr. Marbrino, came downstairs and saw the horrific scene. He spoke quickly in Italian and JJ couldn't quite understand him when the buzzer went off. The police arrived and Mr. Marbrino buzzed them in. Antonio lay lifeless in JJ's arms and the policeman took his pulse. He couldn't find it, but JJ was sure there was one. The officer motioned for JJ to lay Antonio down and then took out a CPR device that enabled him to put air into Antonio's lungs. Air moved his chest and JJ said "Bene," but the officer just looked ahead as he held for a pulse.

Mrs. Torres saw the commotion as she approached for her normal working day. It was a scene she'd lived before and the medics had to stay at the hotel to help calm her down, fearful her heart might falter.

JJ's money was all the intruder took besides Antonio's life. JJ couldn't remember how much but the police insisted he try to remember. He counted the money on him and figured there was around 750,000 lire, $500 U.S., missing. "Many bills of paper?" the police asked.

"Si, mostly 10,000 lire bills."

"That's a pocket full of lira," a policeman said in perfect English as he walked away to report the crime over the radio with the description JJ gave.

Late that afternoon, Ms. Torres asked for JJ by phone from her home. "You go to Bruno and buy there some flowers for Antonio and me." By the time JJ got there, the square was empty and there was no one there to sell flowers. In fact, most of the shops around the square were closed. There was an old wreath of flowers there and JJ propped it back up. He felt too mad to cry and realized he must've been awake while Antonio was murdered.

"I don't know what this means, Bruno, and I don't even know exactly why I'm here. Take care of Antonio and Ms. Torres. They need you." JJ walked out of the back right corner of the square behind the statue, feeling as if he needed a drink. Bourbon was in order, "But where in Roma?" he thought.

The next morning, he went back to the Bruno statue to buy flowers so, when he saw Ms. Torres, he could assure her he'd done it. The mist over the area was gently eerie, as the colors of the fruits and vegetables softened the mood. Some daisies in a bunch were 1,800 lire. He placed them next to the old wreath and looked up into Bruno's face. Dew dripped off of his head as if he, too, was weeping. Emotion came over JJ and he cried as no one paid any attention.

He went across the piazza to an outdoor Caffe Shop for a cup of coffee. He ordered it the way Antonio had made it, with a lot of steamed milk. So much needed to be done, but he felt he had so little mental capacity. He felt like going home. Rome had lost its charm. The young waiter asked him a question he didn't understand and JJ answered "No, gracia," assuming he had asked if he wanted something else since his coffee cup was empty. The waiter smiled and trotted off.

A few minutes later, the boy returned with his father and the man looked at him and said, "My son asked if you minded for I can join you, no?"

"Si, please sit down," JJ said realizing his lack of Italian had put him in a bit of an embarrassing situation. "You have the passion of this piazza and I want to welcome you back often." JJ began to tell him the story of Mrs. Torres sending him to put flowers, and that he wasn't exactly sure why he was there. "You don't know?" he said.

"Well, sir, I know I want to be here."

"Good enough, then," he said sipping his coffee.

"How long have you been in this area?" JJ asked.

"Fifty-nine years. That's my age."

JJ wanted to know more about him. He sat quietly for a moment and was about to ask a question when the elder gentleman started talking.

"You see, I have romance for Roma. My son knows that people enjoy our place here with Bruno there. He wants me to be happy and asks people if his father can join them. I tell stories about history just a little because I feel more surely that someone must represent the present. I was not here with the Romans. There are reminders all over. My son and I are glad for you to be here with us and we want other tourists to feel a part of this old city."

"Thank you. You have such a fantastic city. I'm here because of its past. But you are correct, sir. Today is today. The good with the bad."

"Bruno still cares of you. He helps you. You listen to him. He cares." With that, the old man stood up, toasted toward JJ and said, "Ciao."

JJ walked back to take one of the daisies from the bunch back to Mrs. Torres. Arriving back at the hostel, he placed the flower in a vase and went to get some water for it. In the kitchen, there was a note from Mrs. Torres to the guests saying that the Hotel Raphael nearby had offered to provide breakfast and coffee to her guests for a while. JJ was excited somewhat to be a welcome guest of that beautiful hotel, and planned to go the next day.

Stan, the police investigator, asked for JJ to go look at the mug shots of a group of possible suspects. He took the bus to the station, still carefully watching for the intruder in all places he could on the way there and back.

A day later, there was a tip from one of the local homeless who had seen a bleeding man washing his face in a fountain. He'd seen the man before, so there was enough information to help the police move ahead on their investigation. Antonio's family paid an unexpected visit to Mrs. Torres at the hostel. She was so thankful to them for coming to console her and JJ was touched that, in their own grief, they would reach out to her.

JJ quietly packed to leave for Florence. He heard a knock at the door, then let in the police investigator, who had with him a mug shot of the murderer. JJ was almost sure of it. When the investigator realized JJ was packing, he became concerned.

"Signore, you must not leave. We need you to help us."

"Yes, sir. I'm to meet a friend in Firenze for a week. Then I'm to travel Tuscany. I can keep in touch with you."

"OK, but please do not leave us without talking with us."

Tricia was on her first trip abroad to visit JJ. She had flown into Nice and taken a bus with some friends to Florence. JJ never put much effort into relationships because he seemed to always fall into one. Tricia was young enough to have had only a few boyfriends and her parents weren't aware JJ was one of her professors. So, in a way, she was a bit on the sly with JJ, which suited him fine. Their hotel in Florence was so old that the stairs couldn't handle a big suitcase, so they would raise it by rope from the street below. Tricia was amused slightly (mostly concerned) that JJ might not be in the mood for sex after his nightmare in Rome.

Florence was steeped in romance and beauty. They lay there in the room, talking about how much they missed each other until the hotel called for him to come downstairs. He was met by the local police, asking him to return to Rome immediately to identify a suspect in a lineup. He asked if they could return first thing in the morning, since they had just arrived and were tired. The police agreed, mainly because the trains were running late anyway and, by the time they got to Rome, it would be late.

JJ and Tricia packed their bags and lowered the suitcase by rope to the taxi below which drove them to the train. Flashes of the murderer, frame by frame, ran in JJ's thoughts as the train clackity-clacked on the tracks like an old movie projector running a horror movie over and over in his head. He took some aspirin, worrying he might not be able to identify the murderer. He also kept seeing the Piazza Campo, and the sunlight that made Bruno look alive. This, he thought, means something. "Tricia will enjoy Bruno," he hoped, worrying about her having to deal with the facts of the murder as he would surely be questioned by the police again.

Tricia was upset that their trip to Tuscany was off and was concerned about staying at the hostel. JJ's funds were very low since the robbery and he needed to make some decisions that might be important for Tricia's happiness for the rest of the trip.

The policeman who came to the hotel the morning of the murder met JJ and Tricia at the train station, as expected. JJ spoke in broken Italian so Tricia wouldn't understand his dilemma. The policeman answered he should not worry.

The police station was abuzz. Tricia sat on a bench as JJ was escorted behind closed doors. An hour later, he reappeared and she could tell he looked relieved. It was a positive ID, no mistakes. As they hugged, the policeman came up to them with a smile. "You are to stay at the Hotel Raphael as long as you'd like—they have invited you as their guests," he said.

JJ smiled and knew how much Tricia would enjoy the most picturesque hotel and the area surrounding it. He only worried then what influence the murder would have over her, how well she could adapt to their altered plans and what might happen when she met his friends. He also worried about how much stress the funeral would have on Mrs Torres.

As they arrived in the room, a bottle of champagne and a bouquet of flowers were waiting with a card for Tricia welcoming her to Rome. It was signed by the entire staff of the Hostel Della Pace. "JJ, you're the best person I've ever met. You care more for others than yourself. I want you to take me to Antonio's funeral in the morning."

The next morning Tricia again insisted they both would attend the funeral. JJ felt something intensely emotional for her, something he'd never experienced with a woman before, as all of his worries disappeared in an instant. From that moment on the two were inseparable.

Coat Check—Two Bucks

Try this. Catch the 6:00 P.M. flight to La Guardia from Atlanta. Grab a cab and check into a trendy hotel, say between 45th and 65th. It'll be about 9:00 when your lucky on-time trip gets you into your hotel room. Throw your clothes in closets and drawers and call your friends. They, too, are glad you're on time.

Cab to their place takes 13 minutes and they're on their second bottle of Moët. You head toward the fridge for a beer, but it's too late. They've opened more champagne and you're soon standing there with a flute.

The crackers are picked over now and dinner reservations are pressing, so guzzle up and let's go.

The cab driver pushes the meter and never looks at you as he gets into traffic. His lane changes would cause a pileup in Buckhead that could take hours to fix. He drops you at the front door—any tip will do. The night's still young and he speeds away, the light on his roof is lit and he's lookin' for another customer.

Enter the foyer, check your coat, and get ready for Italian at its best—no wait for food, the owner drops off a plate of antipasti. Bottles of Chianti Reservera are brought one at a time and ice cream for dessert comes on the house. A real credit card experience. Tip 20 percent to the waiter, $2 to the pot as you get your coat, and let's go!

Walking up to the next block will help the cab-catching experience. Cabbie asks the street address of the late-night dance place we named. "Must be cool if he don't know about it," we say.

Wait in a line to get in!? What the hell, the scenery and happenings are worth it. The beat moves through the black walls lining the entry. Two bucks to check your coat, ten bucks house cover charge and dis the salespeople lurking in the entryway to the bar trying to stuff flyers in your hand. It reminds you of the last time you were here, or clubbing in London.

The decorations indicate the owner has a goldmine. Some girl dressed in black with a diamond earring—not in her ear—catches your cologne and throws her head back, nose to the sky, essentially blowing you off like a doe who's caught your scent in the woods. She's obviously into other smells.

The bartender, a muscle jock with a hairdo, wants you to know he's got an attitude and a boyfriend. He bangs your Heineken in front of you hard enough to make suds flow out of the top of the bottle. He turns to ring up the sale. He returns acting like he has not noticed the overflowing green bottle and your change is placed in the pool of spilt beer. You aren't about to just leave it all there though the thought crosses your mind—probably his intention.

You've never heard the song the DJ's playing, or the next one, or the one after that. You dance with conviction, at first with your friends, then by yourself. This would've been a tool (this means not cool) move just a few years ago—still is most places, I suppose.

Guys with gym bodies dance with their shirts tied around their waists, and girls in black dart around them. It's cool to be hot. You can't believe it's 3:30 A.M., and you've just met someone from Chelsea.

The street looks dangerous as you leave the bar; your ears are ringing louder than you can ever remember. Cabs are lined up outside. As you tell your friends "Mañana," your new friend drags you outside and you discuss logistics as you hug and sway. You decide to just get a phone number.

Previous hotel maids' early-morning tapping your door with their master key prompts you to hang the "Don't Disturb" sign out (and you're proud you remembered to do it in your altered state). Falling into bed without taking Tylenol, though, would not be a good idea.

You manage to sleep till noon, then turn on the TV to watch a cartoon you've never heard of. The phone rings and your friends are drinking coffee and rethinking the plans made eagerly in the gusto of last night.

Room service delivers water, OJ and a bagel. You don't care that you're in your boxers as she puts the tray of stuff on the bureau and asks you to sign your name.

"Walking outside feels good," you think, as the sun slips in-between the buildings. Everyone is moving along the sidewalks with somewhere to be, places to go. Not you, not now, nowhere matters. "Cabs will blow their horns for any reason," you think to yourself. "Oh, look at that neat hotel, I wonder how much?" and you pass on by.

Dinner tonight is just starting to circle your thoughts, as the morning's bagel wears thin. It'll be a small French restaurant you've learned about from one of your clients. The friends you'll be taking haven't been, either.

After dinner you go back to the hotel and sleep. In the morning, it'll be a quick trip downstairs for breakfast.

The corned beef hash is unlike anywhere in the South, and you recognize a couple of the older waiters from past breakfast times.

You have just enough time to go down to Madison Avenue to pick out a new tie and cologne no one at home has. You're into a new look and smell now.

The guy next to you on the plane home nods his head to the music he's listening to and you're glad to feel up to a rum drink when you get back to the house. You'll call up some friends and go to the local joint for a burger instead of cooking anything from the freezer. They hear the stories, ask some questions and, after a while, you're back home eyeing the covers on your bed and the landing pad they protect. Pulling them back, you slither underneath the sheets and it sure feels good to be in your own bed again. Until, that is, restlessness calls you North once more to sniff the bouquet of a New York night.

After Omaha

Something's happened in town. The church bell is ringing and it's not Sunday. Georges runs inside to see his mother's reaction because he's never heard the bell ring, except on Sundays.

He sees the concern on her face as she tells him to run to town. It's about two miles, and Georges prefers to go barefoot because his boots are too cumbersome. At seventeen, your soles are tough.

He starts fast and slows about halfway. A minute later he's in town with the others, heading toward the church. The bell is still ringing. The men ahead are huddled and the news will soon be dispersed. He's not sure if he's old enough to join the huddle, so he stops to speak to Madame Fouchart. She's a short woman, solid in every way.

"Mother sent me," Georges says to her.

Through a blank stare she responds, matter-of-factly, "Yes, but she'll be here, too."

"What's up?" a curious Georges asks. Madame simply stared ahead, arms folded, her hair brushing her eyebrows with the wind gusts. He obliged by being quiet. The group dispersed and William Tibeie, Madame Fouchart's oldest brother, headed over to them.

Sure enough, William reported Georges' mother *was* almost there. She'd put on a clean dress and pulled her hair back, since it hadn't been washed.

One of the men caught Madame's eye, confirming her worst fear.

"Oh no, dear God . . . war," Madame said, after interpreting the glimpse. Georges was just then catching his breath as his heart slowed its pace. But not for long. Georges was the perfect age to go off and defend his country against conflict. Realization swept his face as his mother was debriefed. He could see her looking at him and then, in an instant, she bolstered herself to approach him with her "put on your boots—there's stuff to do" message. This calmed Georges' racing imagination about as long as people could ignore crying babies in church. This was a moment where no one but a father could assuage—and Georges' father was busy at the boatyard in Best, near Charborge. In vain, his mother tried her best to fill his shoes. When he was away, she usually adapted, but no mother could prepare a son for war with ease.

Georges felt a tug on his arm as he was pulled aside by one of the farmers, a family friend. The man's deep voice, with a time-worn country French annunciation, bellowed a beautiful melody from his pink and violet lips and tongue. He drooled more than Georges would have liked; Georges had learned from experience it's only bad when you get too close in front. From that vantage, you'll certainly get wet.

"Georges," continued the excited farmer, "these women are worried sick over you now. You must not let them get carried away with this." With that Georges nodded as his thoughts were turned down to simmer and his attention turned to his mother.

Georges and his mother walked home in utter silence. Both were afraid to say anything and, each time one or the other thought of something to say, like a game of chess, they were preoccupied with the pending result of the other's move.

Georges was the only one of the dozen or so young men from his small village to survive the war. His injuries would, however, hinder him greatly. His handicapped condition warmed up his many friendships from the town, and the countryside. He never married, although his handicap didn't seem to stop women from tempting him with the thought. He had a clever mind, so his business dealings provided him with food and he gave money to the church when he could.

The cemetery population grew larger than the town's population by the time Georges was forty-five. When he became ill, there were always people to care for him. He did not like that ruckus, though, and once nearly died because he wouldn't let anyone know if he was sick.

Not many felt sorry for him because of how happily he lived. His smiles and quick wit made people happy. Once, while visiting his parents' graveside, he heard a newly widowed woman speaking of purchasing a marker for her husband's grave. After her continued indecision, he interjected, "Oh heavens, Marie, he's been dead six months! How can you be so sure he cares that much?" Both she and the priest chuckled and she made a decision.

With no siblings, Georges was curious who'd take responsibility to bury him so he went to Father Baker on his 91st birthday. "Father, my mother planned my funeral the day we stood outside hearing the news of war. I guess, in that regard, my burial has been discussed enough. But it hadn't occurred to me until the past year that, at my age, I had better make a plan. God's been good to me and I'm not sure I ever figured out what exactly His plan for me was. War is bad. Maybe I'm a reminder to all of just that. Planting teenagers in the ground is not a good idea. But the good earth has accepted her share exponentially because of conflict. The children of my fellow servicemen should look at the military cemetery and not only see who died, but mourn also for the ones never born and feel grateful for their own lucky lives."

"Georges, your life is most remarkable. As for your death, that sad day has been contemplated with gifts to the church since the war by so many people I can't even count. Most every will and testament leaves the church some money with you in mind. Just as the ringing of our bell reminds us of the time of day, the joy of marriage, or a pending worship service, the sound reminds you of the day war loomed over your life. Your body does remind us all of how treacherous wars can be. Your friends who died would be proud of the way you have lived."

Georges paused for a long time, his mind surely drifting through painful remembrances of a war that ripped him from youth. He finally gazed up at Father Baker. He cleared his throat and proclaimed, "I suppose if you're going to keep collecting on those bequests, I'm worth more to you living. Avec moi, s'il vous plaît, let's have some sherry."

Raining Rum

The weather began to fail and the barometer directly fell. Seas were sloppy. The wind gained speed. The swells were getting larger and their tops were all white. The water turned black as the daylight turned to dark. The sails were spilling the gusty air as their edges fluttered with great noise. The rigging pulled tight and made horrible sounds. The first mate ordered more sails furled to keep the gale-force winds from harming the ship. The crew knew they were in danger. Their captain was drunk and sleeping off his latest bottle of rum in his cabin down below. The big ship began to plow downward as the ocean became furious. The stern of the ship was sticking high into the air so that, from the helm, the view of the rest of the ship was downward. The rain started falling sideways if you can call sideways falling. Water covered the decks and the storm was in control. The mate ordered all remaining sails reefed to keep them from being torn away from the ship by the blowing gale.

The ship lay sideways to the seas, being beaten starboard by the weather. "Wake the captain," the first mate ordered, knowing he would have awakened by now if he wasn't drunk. A hint of fear cracked in his shout, but the order sifted through the gaining speed of the deafening wind. The crew knew the captain would be their best hope for safety. His tenure at sea dated back farther than most of his peers. He'd experienced this before and survived. His seamanship was well documented— his personality totally misunderstood.

The second mate returned to deck looking somewhat confused, however he nodded to indicate the captain was on his way. A big hat on his head, a heavy weather coat, untied boots and a bottle of rum in hand, Captain Molony topped the hatch holding onto the rigging. Immediately, the hat was blown from his head, held by the straps choking him as it danced around his head. Not particularly bothered by the distraction, he looked up and saw the sails furled just as a wave crashed from overhead, sending a wall of water on deck that pounced on top of the captain and crew. This was a popular way men were lost at sea . . . swept overboard by the rage of a storm.

As the water disappeared, the crew looked up to see a bottle of rum and a hand sticking up out of the hatch. Captain Molony jumped up on deck and took a swig.

He walked aft without holding on, the boat rocking violently, and grabbed the tiller. "Raise the mizzen and give me some goddamn sails!" he bellowed. The stunned crew hopped into action. They feared him worse than the outcome of his order, which they feared would surely tear the sails from the rigging once they were unfurled.

He slowly turned the ship downwind and got some headway. "Where the hell are we?" he shouted. The mate answered him with precise coordinates captured earlier from the sextant.

"Then get those men below before they get hurt. Leave me two sailors. Brave sorts . . . and bring fresh rum. This shit's gotten salty!" he shouted referring to the bottle of rum in his hand. As the men ducked below deck out of the weather and imminent danger, they wondered if they would ever see him again.

"These men have volunteered, sir, and I'll stay also," the first mate said pointing to two sailors.

"You get below, they may need you. Boys, let's get our arses in control of this mess," he said with a slight smile and a sharp eye. The two young men appeared poised with conviction.

"Move fast on deck, and always know where to go for cover. We're gonna trim for a reach—it'll be tough sailing. Don't get your hair caught in the sheets," he said with a grin and a belly-shaking chuckle. Obviously, he had seen it happen before. "In fact, c'mon o'here, son," he said motioning to the sailor with long hair. He drew his knife from under his coat, and in one move without holding on to anything but a bunched handful of hair, his sharp knife took off most of the young man's blonde excess. And again he chuckled as the sailor headed toward the bow happy to have his life and not too worried about his new look.

The captain caught a wave and surfed it until the ship began to turn on it's own into the wind. The sails began to luff furiously. "Trim those sails," he yelled. They couldn't hear him, but knew what to do. Their arms bulged as the two men struggled to pull in the sheet to stop the intense shaking caused by the loud luffing of their only raised sail.

Lashing the tiller secure with a rope, the captain ran up the lee deck to the two sailors. "On three," the captain shouted—they grabbed rope and pulled. It worked and the ship began to list, and finally the sail caught the wind and they began to make headway again.

The water was knee-deep on deck as the passing waves crashed by. The captain made his way back to the tiller and held it with all his might. The sails frayed on the edges, but held up and the ship beat its way through the weather. Hours passed.

The captain opened his eyes, red from the salt water, to see his two sailors heading his way. They were bringing the rum bottle, which had amazingly survived the ordeal so far. The weather was breaking, though ever so slightly. The captain took a good look at them, guzzled a slug, then handed them the bottle. "You sailors save this. I've had enough," he said as the big ship still tossed through remnants of the storm. "We're not safe just yet," he said as he took slack out of the rope tied to his tiller. "There will be a time soon to celebrate, just hang in there."

The next few hours fell by slowly as the aged storm slowly died. The captain was half conscious as he tried to maintain headway. Soon, he felt someone shaking him. "Captain, I'll take over now," the first mate said. The captain stood up trying to maintain his footing, shook the water from his hat and slowly walked toward the hatch. The crew had come up from below and, one by one, quietly congratulated and thanked the captain for guiding them to safety. He avoided their eyes. He knew they were sincere. As he approached the hatch amidships, he stopped and turned to the crew. They all watched. He gestured for his two assistants to step forward. Holding the rum bottle arm in arm, they approached the captain. He stood up tall and saluted them. Then, he saluted the others.

Once below, he neatly hung his foul weather gear and began picking up his things, which had fallen to the deck from the storm. A painted picture of his girlfriend lay faceup, as if she wished to be held. "Not now," he growled at her out loud, stumbling to wash the layers of salt from his face. Rubbing his hairy face with a towel, he caught a glimpse of himself. He stared thinking, "Who is that person?"

"Why can't you settle down?" he hissed into the mirror. He grabbed the fallen picture with a shaking hand and hurled it toward the wall. The sound of breaking glass made him wince.

He collapsed onto his bunk and pulled the cork from some half-full whiskey bottle and took a big gulp. With the brown liquor coursing down his slightly sore throat, causing a stinging sensation, it leaked from the corners of his water-logged mouth as he collapsed to sleep.

As exhaustion overcame consciousness, the masculine aroma of salt water and strong whiskey drenched the cabin. Only the occasional moonlight through the small porthole saw the captain's salt-stained cheeks.

At the end of this voyage, a sobered captain and his girl reacquainted. Their relationship would be different now, yet, in some way it seemed as a natural progression of their days and months together. Had she finally tamed the giant? Commitment was something you did physically, he thought. Emotionally, he found effortless commitment well.

They did marry. A new family was his conviction, his life now as soothing as Monet's lilies painted upon the face of a future just beginning. His children would find him a loving and gentle father, stern with his feelings, then gentlemanly playful with their children, too, many years later. A long life for the captain was the reward of a lifetime of good luck.

Preacher, I Need a Doctor

Malita Hendricks grew up in a small town in Arkansas until she was 12. At which time, her father got work in Dallas and they moved. After a few years she met her beau, Maurice. Maurice was from Houston and they would live there to raise their family. There was plenty of good work in Houston in those days.

Maurice died at the age of 79. Malita was financially secure enough to move or travel, but preferred to live in the house and bake pound cakes for the grandchildren—Maw Maw, they called her.

Ten years later, Maw Maw was well in her 80s and fit as a falcon. She still drove her old Dodge each week to the grocery and, on Sunday, to the Baptist church downtown. Maurice was quite active in the church in his day, but other men were there now and Maurice was mostly forgotten.

Malita Hendricks gave flowers for the altar each year in his memory and the preacher would usually make special mention of the former vestryman. This year, Preacher Mullins was too ill to be there and Mr. Segart preached.

"Don't be idle in your religion. Be a Christian by giving yourself to the church," Segart began. "Like great parishioners before you, including Maurice Hedrick (Malita cringed at the mispronunciation of their family name) for whom flowers are given in memory of." Few people were there who knew her, but a couple did know where her usual pew was and turned to look over at her.

Her friends were old. Many had already died. Her preacher was too sick to preach anymore and she wasn't sure she wanted to trust her soul

130

to some young bible-slapping man of the cloth who couldn't pronounce her name.

All week she thought and read her bible, while asking God what to do. Sounds from the church came to mind and she would hum them as her maid ironed sheets. "You know, Isabel, I have outlived my friends and my preacher may as well be dead 'cause he can't preach," she said. Isabel, a longtime helper at their home, spoke up.

"No, miz Hendricks, you don't wishes nobody be dead."

"No, but I don't even like my doctor. Ever since Dr. Salter died, I can't seem to get the right medicine. I'm so stove up all the time, I can hardly get dressed anymore. I think I'll drive in and see Preacher Mullins. He's been so good to me and I know I should go. He likes persimmons. Isabel, are the persimmons ready to pick?"

"Yes'um. I'll go gets 'um."

Malita fired up the Dodge and drove into town. As the old slant-six hummed its way through familiar intersections, Malita relaxed her grip on the wheel and wistfully recalled details of the man she was about to see. Pete Mullins had become quite a figure in Houston's political community due to his frequent convocations of new facilities, various committee appointments and the high-profile funerals he would preside over. His style was well received by Texans, even though he was not a native himself. He could grieve for the departed with simple, powerful words. Baptisms were always cheerful and his gentle ways were usually well received by the babies being baptized, too.

He had pioneered parishioners through the changes that filtered their way into the church over time. Malita thought it especially profound that he preached of acceptance and tolerance and was even close to the Jewish community because of his focus on the universal love of God. This set him apart from the norm and she'd admired him greatly.

The Dodge sputtered up the long drive to the ailing preacher's sprawling residence, owned by the church. Even the two-story brick house looked a bit ill. It needed paint and the grass was bare in too many places. The shrubs hadn't been chopped recently and grew in all directions, even into the walkways. As Malita walked up to the house, she had to push them aside to keep them from snagging her stockings.

Multiple coats of old paint covered the doorbell and it looked inoperable. She decided to push it anyway and waited a minute to see if anyone came to the door. As she did she recalled that, in her younger days, she would've heard the eminent ring from inside.

After a brief wait, the door opened. It was Carey, the housekeeper. "Hello, Carey," Malita began, "I've come to visit."

"Yes, Miz Malita, do comes in," she said politely and held open the green door. The house inside was clean and smelled of furniture polish. "I'll tell the Reverend youz here," Carey said taking the bag of persimmons from her. Malita escorted herself into the living room and sat down on the couch looking over the tastefully arranged pictures of his family.

From the corner of her eye she could see Mr. Mullins entering. "Oooohhh, Malita," he said with his great voice that had preached to her for over 45 years. "So nice for you to come visit an old goofball like me," he said.

"Now, Pete," Malita retorted, "you might be an old preacher, but never a goofball. How are you? I've missed you in church."

"Well, Malita, I've been having spells pert reg-lar now. I don't know when I might feel faint, so I've been at home a lot. I seem to get along well here. The kids stop by for cookies, and your visit makes me happy as a clam!"

Their small talk continued for an hour as he entertained Malita in his grand, eloquent way. Carey served tea with all the goodies as Mr. Mullins told some stories. One of the women's auxiliary groups, he said, had been debating whether they should purchase a plaque honoring Miss Sutton for her effort in tending to the choir robes, or one honoring Mrs. Winton Dukes for her help with the refreshments at Sunday school. The thought of heated arguments over robes and refreshments brought Malita such laughter that tears rolled down her cheeks.

"Pete, I don't like being old," Malita blurted.

"No, Malita. Nor do I." He paused as he sat back in his chair, rubbing the arms of it with his hands.

"Can I leave God out of this for a moment?" he asked, much to her surprise.

"Yes, if you must," she said gallantly.

"The world spins about with persons brought to, and taken from, life every waking tick of the clock," began the Reverend. "I used to tell my elderly parishioners that it was God who chose. I would confront them with what they needed to hear and, I have no regrets about that. Now, I'm getting old, too, and I can hear the doubts I've had more than the message. Is that fair? No, but I have to understand. We had our lives, Malita, and it was all in the simple things. Good lives too, I'd say. Memories search minds and vice versa. When you are asked to pull out remembrances of great times, your mind takes over and goes for the excitement dictated by society. That, unfortunately, is natural. But you know, all of a sudden I've remembered some things that never seemed worth much memory. A child looked at me once, as I visited his elementary school, and asked, 'Are you gonna talk to us about the devil?' Think of that. His only thought was that a preacher put down evil. Another time I pulled the car into a filling station in Pine Bluff. An old attendant smiled at us as if we were his only customers. He was pleasant and interested in our well-being. A young man drove in while we were there, and gave some fresh fruit to him. Oh, thank you, by the way, for my favorite fruit. Carey will conjure up some persimmons for me just like I like them, with lots of vanilla ice cream! Anyway, I was curious at first, but then he patted the young man on his back and said thank you. I never needed to know the circumstances of that situation at the fillin' station. I learned a lot, though."

"Malita," he continued, "I've still all the faith, if not more, that I've ever had. The Lord always challenges us and it's the faith that keeps us going. I enjoyed my trips to Europe, Latin America and the conventions in the U.S., but I see many interesting faces here at home. Faces of the homeless at my church on cold winter mornings, faces of those saying their vows with love and those just trying to impress parents. Faces of groomsmen, rosy from the drinks they've had, and the little children dressed up to throw flowers. Flowers are impressive in themselves, Malita. Did you see the Easter flowers this year? Weren't they simply sensational! They help us remember. It is the real memories that you and I can relate to."

Preacher Mullins continued, now addressing Malita directly. "You want everything to stay as it was—so do I. But that can't be. It just must change and it will always change. What should not change are the *pleases* and *thank yous*, the *I love yous*, the *can I help yous* . . . and so on. Our ears hear this kind of language more in Great Britain where they don't take their own language for granted. There you hear great words that have been ingrained in their culture for hundreds of years. They seem to mean it! When I asked directions to the Tower of London one day, a paperboy pointed us on our way. He smiled, bounced a bit and said, 'Cheers!' How sweet that voice still is in my memories."

There was quite a pause in their talking. It wasn't an uncomfortable pause, though. "Well, Malita, I wonder what you really might have on your mind to bring you all the way over here to visit me?"

"I've forgotten, Pete. Like always, you've pacified and enriched me to no end." Malita no longer had those feelings that had compelled the visit to see him. Once home, she peeled herself a ripe persimmon and lobbed on some ice cream.

When word came that Preacher Mullins died several months later, Malita sent a basket of fresh fruit to the funeral parlor with a card saying, simply, "Cheers."

He Went to Paris (Finally)

The Land of Beautiful Language was alive with shops and pedestrians eager to look and be seen. I am here and I'm to absorb what is the essence of their city. I have not felt intimidation since I left home.

Common thought seems passé to me now that I can look into the expressions on their faces. Why do they all seem so confident in their presence? Their ancient city gives them a reminder that perhaps they will relinquish their footprints on the cobblestone streets to others who will yearn to know what their own lives are about.

The old lady looked so peaceful as she eagerly helped with directions while we looked to find the perfect Thanksgiving lunch. "Bag lady," my friend said. No. I saw a young girl on the Avenue des Armenu in the 1940s watching the U.S. troops, telling herself that, no matter how much loss of pride she might endure, she'd vow to help wayward Americans like me till she couldn't. That's what I saw in this short woman's face. She'd have taken my remuneration straight to the church.

Pretty people with smiles and thoughtfulness. The doorman at the hotel, the waitress at the café, Christofer, a busboy, and friends Terrell, John, and Alexander. Why am I so lucky and seem to recognize it only to a small degree?

Iron Man

In 1963, Marcus McTween was on a mission. He was in the mood to learn of, and see, his father's history. Collecting his thoughts, he engineered a strategy he was certain would fail. He started by writing to the Parisian company his deceased father had worked for before, and during, the German occupation.

Not expecting a reply was his way of proceeding. He didn't get one. Meanwhile, he looked through old letters and found an address that appeared to be his father's home during the 10 years he spent in Paris. He wrote to the "Current Resident" as follows:

> *Dearest Amis,*
>
> *My father lived at your address from 1936-1946. He died last year and I'm eager to visit Paris. He loved it so much. His trade was iron working and he did the best in our area of Ireland during his lifetime. I am a doctor, and my sister is married with four children. None of us have been to Paris. I hope this letter greets warm hands. Please write to me if it will be possible to visit your home, and if you or someone may have information on David McTween.*
>
> *Sinc.*
>
> *M. McTween*

The letter was replied to, as follows:

Dear Mr. M. McTween,

You must call me at my office before you attempt to visit the homestead. My frail mother lives there alone. I hope for you to understand.

My office telephone is 47 44 98 46.

We are happy to greet you.

Sinc.

Silvia Roistra

Marcus was 41 then, and he would travel alone since he couldn't afford to bring his wife. His sister, Julia, to the best of her memory, wrote down a very detailed history of what their father had done while in Paris.

Dearest Brother,

As you go to visit father's home in Paris, I've a few things for you to know from my memories and talks with mother. Dad left Ireland and traveled to England to learn the trade of iron working. Our uncle, a blacksmith, had recommended this. He lasted only a few months, since most of the business was with residential customers. There was a major restoration going on in Paris, and he was needed. He arrived in either 1935 or 1936. His first job was for one year, then he joined the French of the Seine where he worked for almost 10 years. The first job was with Mr. Eric Amstrofnor, Mother says. His second job and home address you know. He frequented a brasserie near to the Bastille, called Luchene and made friends with the Pochet family (Hildred and Jean visited years ago) and the Chenocois. Mother said she looks like Aunt Bula, but can't remember her name. Please take pictures for our scrapbooks.

Sinc.

Your loving sister, Julia

The streets of Paris were busy, even though it was 11:00 P.M.. Marcus took the luggage from the bus and walked toward a small hotel he had chosen to stay in. A pub appeared and he stopped for a beer. The next four blocks were tough on him and left him out of breath, despite his fit appearance.

The next day, he walked to the old foundry where his father had worked. A flower shop and a furniture store crammed with junk they called antiques, had replaced the foundry. The retail area was called Foundry Place. He asked at the antiques store, but no one knew of the old foundry.

The flower shop owner was out for lunch, so he headed to the Bastille Monument. It was so innocent, poking up into the sky. He saw a brasserie nearby and went inside to inquire of the Luchene.

"This is it," a young waiter answered. Marcus sat down at a table near the windows and began to talk about his father having been a frequent customer many years earlier.

"My grandfather worked here," the waiter said. After a while, they had enjoyed a couple of cafés and the young man promised to ask his grandfather if he knew of a McTween. Marcus would be back in a day or so.

Later that afternoon, he met Gertrude. She was the "flower lady" and knew all about the foundry because her father, the owner of the foundry, was still alive at 93. He'd received Marcus' letter and wanted him to visit. Problem was, he lived in Versailles. Marcus said he'd go there and they planned lunch on Friday for his rendezvous.

"Your father never got over the deportation of the Jews," Gertrude said. "His friends were lost. He watched as one of his best friends was taken from our foundry by the Germans. We all watched as he was escorted out of the building."

"My father's best friend?"

"Oui."

"What was his name?"

"Abe Marcus."

"Marcus? We never heard of him."

"No?"

"Are you sure? Your name is Marcus, Oui?"

"Oui."

The next day, Marcus called Silvia Roistra. She was excited to show Marcus the home of her mother, who'd inherited the place from her father, Mr. McTween's landlord.

"Mrs. Marchey is eager to meet you," Silvia said as they wandered into the courtyard. She was waiting at the door and greeted Marcus with kisses and a home full of wonderful aromas.

"Your father did all of this," she said as she waved her hand toward the benches, the ironwork on the windows and a marvelous sculpture.

"He did all of this?"

"Oui."

"This statue?"

"Oui."

"Who is it?"

"A Jewish friend."

"Is his name Marcus?"

"Possibly, I can't remember."

"He lived here, in this room. He was a wonderful friend to my husband. We were sad to see him leave and I am sorry for you he passed on." Marcus took several rolls of pictures of the work and enjoyed the hospitality of warm and friendly hosts.

The train ride to Versailles displayed some interesting landscapes mixing the old with the new. Flowers and small yards nestled between run-down sheds and old concrete foundations. The walk outside the Versailles train station was crowded with tourists going to see the palace. He was greeted with an openness Paris didn't appear to have.

Walking through the market, with vegetables and bric-a-brac cluttered in little areas, Marcus saw the restaurant ahead. The maitre d' was there to turn away tourists, making room for the locals only. He greeted Marcus and took him to a table where two gentlemen sat with a large carafe of red wine and near-empty glasses.

"Bonjour."

"Bonjour," responded Marcus who then sat down.

And the broken French from Marcus gave way to better English from Mr. Armstrofner. After the usual discussion of family and travel conditions, Marcus set the stage.

"Dad was proud of his life in Paris, but never wanted to return. He wanted his memories to stay as they were. Mother thought he left your company, Mr. Armstrofner, to work elsewhere.

"Marcus, I remember many things as if they happened this morning, yet some are quite vague. Your father worked for me over 10 years. He had a second job, too. He taught at the Academy. He made more money there in the end. His works sold well."

"Works?"

"Oui, his sculptures, you know."

"No sir, we don't know about that."

"No?"

"Not at all."

Amstrofner spoke in French to his friend Mr. Lawrence. They nodded to each other after a while, and he continued with Marcus.

"Well, he kept me busy in the foundry with his iron working. People all over Paris hired us to fabricate ironwork. We restored the iron at Notre Dame, mainly because of your father."

"That's not surprising to me. He loved his trade."

"Your father befriended a young man and convinced me to hire him."

"Abe Marcus."

"You know?"

"Not much. Gertrude mentioned him."

"Abe became the best ironworker I'd ever had. Your father liked teaching him so well he took the offer to work at the Academy. He was a great teacher."

"Gertrude said the Germans . . . "

Mr. Armstrofner held up his hand to stop Marcus. He asked his friend Mr. Lawrence to pour some more wine and he took a big sip.

"Monsieur, let me tell you I have tried to forget that day every day since. I have not spoken of that day except in confidence with God. But I want you to hear me and hope I don't upset you. I don't expect forgiveness." He was remarkable for his age and Marcus felt bad for rushing him into this conversation. He was visibly shaken as he took some more of the wine into his mouth with just a slight slurping sound mixing the air with the wine much like a shining carburetor on a finely tuned engine.

"The war was demanding on me with the requests for different items. The German officers would come to my place and threaten my family just to get their enjoyment. They came in one day and asked me if I had any Jews working. I said I did not. But I knew Abe was Jewish. And he was the only one. They threatened to close down my foundry if they found out I was lying . . . " He lost his ability to speak momentarily, fighting back a choking that couldn't be completely suppressed. After a while he said, "Your father never forgave me. We never spoke . . . " and he choked up again.

"Monsieur McTween, I never knew your father until after the war," Mr. Lawrence said.

"I want to invite you to come to my home now. We'll drop Eric off at his home first."

They rode in Mr. Lawrence's BMW to a nice building which housed Mr. Armstrofner's apartment. Not much was said during the trip. As Armstrofner was helped by the doorman, he turned to Marcus and said, "This watch is the watch I got for your father when he completed 10 years with my company. I want you to have it. He, your father, refused it."

Marcus took the paper bag and, looking inside, he found the original box. It was a beautiful gold pocket watch. Inscribed inside were his initials. Briefly, Marcus thought of refusing it, too, but he realized how much it meant to Mr. Armstrofner.

"Our family will be so excited to receive this and the story behind it, sir."

With that, he turned with the help of the doorman and walked inside of his apartment building. There was so much left unsaid, Marcus thought. "Marcus, you might think you could've learned more from him, but I can tell you that you just got the part he's been afraid to say to anyone before. Now, I will take you to show you the rest of what you should know."

Mr. Lawrence pulled up to the gate in front of a building and it opened. This was his home. A beautiful chateau, landscaped with wonderful gardens along the drive up to the loggia.

"Gracious. This is magnificent."

"Merci. Marcus, your father taught iron working at the Academy. In his spare time, he made sculptures. Many of them are here. I consider his works to be quite good and there is a fair price fetched if one comes for sale."

"Really? It seems odd he didn't mention it."

"He stopped with his statue of Abe. That was his final work."

"The one at his home in Paris . . . "

"Oui. That's the one. But look at these in the foyer and the gardens. They are meant to be together."

Marcus looked at each one. Touching the exterior with softness, he remembered with mumbling affirmation. "Do these each have names?"

"Oui, I've catalogued them with pictures. I've a copy for you."

"There, what's that?"

"*Family*, it's called. We never knew why. He just loved it and would visit me to see it. Possibly, it's you and your sister, Abe, and your mother. Only your father could've planned his parenthood so well."

Marcus looked over and over the sculptures, then at artwork collected in the beautiful home. His eyes were wet with emotion, yet his heart was burning with a mischievous beat.

"Mr. McTween, I have crated a sculpture I want to send to your mother. Please give me the address and I will arrange for it to be delivered right away. It should be there soon after you return home. Tell her that your father gave it to me since I was such a good customer. In his appreciation for my collecting his works, he wanted me to have this special work. Once I saw it I knew why," he said. "He just wouldn't consider taking any francs for it. I know your family should have this piece."

As they said good-byes at the train station, Marcus dreamed he'd just left the royal palace and Louis XIV himself had put the mysterious statue crate on his carriage, bid him farewell and watched as the horses galloped away with the treasure strapped tightly on.

Back in Paris, Marcus went back to the brasserie for a beer. "Monsieur, how are you?" the young man said. "My grandfather's mad at me for not knowing who your father is. He's the one who did all of this beautiful iron work."

"It doesn't surprise me that he remembered my father. I just returned from Versailles and found a collection of his work there. I am speechless. We never knew about it," Marcus said.

"Grandfather sent you this letter! He said he would like to buy you some drink, so have all you want!" He tucked the letter unopened in his coat pocket, ordered a beer and began telling about the collection in Versailles.

Marcus never remembered a better time drinking. Oh, sure, he'd been drunk plenty of times. But you know those certain occasions, when you're already buzzed from enthusiasm, when even the slightest drink brings intoxication. And a few too many were in order.

The day was half over when Marcus was awakened by the noise in the hallway. "Gosh," he thought, "I've lots to do before I go home. More pictures of the statue at his homestead, pictures of the foundry and a visit to the Academy." He quickly was dressed and on the street, making time for a café. After the jolt of caffeine, he packed to go home. It was time to go reveal the secrets to his family of the father they loved. He decided to wait and read the letter he'd been given at Luchene until the entire family was together, and safely packed it in his luggage.

The family all gathered at Marcus' mother's home. Full of excitement, they opted to read the letter first. Marcus opened it and began interpreting, for it was written in French.

> *Dear Son McTween,*
>
> *When I first met your elder, he was handsome and eager to succeed. His dreams will never leave my thoughts. His accomplishments were far exceeding his dreams.*
>
> *There were times when he was closer to me than my family. We grew up with many experiences. He always knew he'd come back to see us when he left. The funny thing is that we all knew he wouldn't.*
>
> *He loved life more through a good laugh, projected emotion with a sad thought, and offered more of himself to his friends than they to him. He could cry and smile at the same time. Confucius said something about that, but I forgot what!*

It never occurred to me his son would come to visit. I hope you will return often. Do know there's love here for him. May he rest forever in the peace he lived in.

Looking up at his family, he just shook his head.

"I'm afraid we've been had," Marcus said.

"What do you mean, Marcus?" his wife asked.

"Dad was more worldly than we knew. He yearned to let us feel that. We barely noticed. And now, we're learning from total strangers of his heart."

"Let's open the crate!" one of the children blurted.

"Well, Mother? What do you think is in there?" Marcus asked.

"It certainly is of the person who confused him the most. He never understood or related to his own father, who died a month after your father returned from France. His father was stern, I'll tell you. That sculpture could be of his father."

The family all watched as Uncle Carl opened the box. He pried the wooden boards off one at a time as they squeaked and popped in resistance to the force. As the wrapping paper was pulled off of the object, it was apparent Grandma was wrong. It was the sculpture of an old boat. It was beautiful and they all looked at the elder Mrs. McTween. She stared without a word.

"Well, Mother?" her daughter Julia asked. "Are you disappointed? It's just a boat."

"No," she sighed, "That's a replica of the old ferry. No wonder . . ."

"What? No wonder what?"

And she sat quietly staring at the beautiful bronze ferry boat, with thoughts running through her head.

"That's the Hoploca Ferry," she finally said in a quiet voice.

"The one that sank, the one that killed so many people?" Julia asked.

"Your father lost his best childhood friend when the ferry sank . . . he never got over it. The pain he must have gone through to do this . . ."

The family agreed to donate the sculpture to the local museum in honor of those who died. The day of the unveiling, when it was officially placed in the exhibition area, a large crowd of local people came to see it. They, too, were touched.

Marcus wrote to Mr. Lawrence and explained the story of the boat sinking. He also gave the name of the museum, which had an interest in acquiring other works if they were available.

Many years later, the museum received a package from Versailles. It was a sculpture named *Father* and was gifted from the estate of the late Mr. Lawrence.

Tale by the Sea

Michelle moved from the farming hills of Provence to the coast. Her cooking was quite good and she found summer work in the restaurants. Doing so allowed her to live all year in her flat without roommates. A sign of prosperity.

Summer of the third year she was offered a position on a new yacht, the sailing vessel *Avalon*, built in Holland of the finest teak. Though she was a little unsure of sailing, she took the position hoping she would like it. The new boat was 151 feet long and considered the finest built in many years. The owner often said, "1926 was a good year to launch a yacht."

While working on the *Avalon* she met her husband, Phillipe. Phillipe, at that time, was the first mate on a motor yacht, the *Empress*, owned by an Italian family. She often hoped the two would work on the same boat but it never happened. Raising children seemed more important anyway, so she retired to begin a family. She and Phillipe had four children together.

The small fishing village of St. Tropez seemed a likely place to call home and they made it their home. It was also the location for Monique's (the first daughter of three children to marry) wedding.

The church in town was alive that day. Michelle looked beautiful and was every bit as graceful as the passengers she had cooked for ever were. Her friends took notice of her happiness and, at the end of the affair, they eased her back to earth by naming her Guest of Honor at tea for ten.

Phillipe had good sense for investing in small properties. With his salary increase after becoming captain of the *Empress*, he was able to afford to continue his acquisitions. Michelle was consulted each time, a courtesy not typical in the Mediterranean.

"Phillipe, can we find a nice property on Cap-Ferrat?" Michelle asked on Bastille Day, 1940.

"You've always liked that place," he said to her.

"Oui, let's go visit again soon," she said almost in a pleading voice. He agreed that, upon the next trip where there was room for her aboard the *Empress*, they would go. However, property there was very expensive and they both feared it would be impossible to find something affordable.

It took years for the trip to happen due to the war. The *Empress* was sold to some British families and, after six months, Phillipe resigned to work for a perfumer from England on his yacht, the *Hamptonesse*. The yacht was built in a small English shipyard. Her engines were the latest in diesels and yielded fantastic speed. The lines were quite smart and she gathered a crowd at every port.

Michelle wore a linen dress to dinner the first night in the port of Nice. She had beautiful skin and was lucky to keep her tan with minimal exposure. Her presence was charming, and her simple dress and style were envied by women with dangling armor and painted faces. Even when completely unnerved, she looked as graceful as a bold flag in a 10-knot breeze.

Phillipe looked masculine and proper in his uniform of blue and gold. His white gloves spoke of his clean ship. His humor glided well among boarders and his glance was as powerful as most stares. Seated across from Phillipe and Michelle were Mr. and Mrs. Rottingham of New York and Dr. and Mrs. Henry Walker of Charleston, South Carolina (in those days, it was quite fashionable to have American guests).

The owner and his wife shared opposite table ends and the servers were timely with their presentations so as not to interrupt any conversation. Michelle could avoid being the center of attention better than most who aspired to be in that position. However, there had to be some discussion of her, otherwise it would've been crass.

"Tell me, Michelle, how you two met," was a simple enough inquiry to which Michelle could expound and her answer was hopefully enough to quench their curiosity.

"You see, I'm from the farming county of Provence," she said with such interesting, almost eloquent, English with the lilt of a lovely accent. "We were often in similar ports on our different boats, I was a cook . . . "

"A chef," Phillipe added.

"Whatever, mind you, and there was a young man on another boat and we were talking one day and then I knew that if he wished for me then OK. He was often waving at me, which really warmed my chest and heart, and as they say 'the rest is history.'"

Mrs. Rottingham quickly demanded, "Which port?"

At the same time they answered differently. Michelle said "Monte Carlo" and Phillipe said "Genova." After a brief discussion in French, Michelle conceded that it must have been Genova. "Oh, he's right. I forgot!" she said almost blushing. "Why had you not reminded me before?" Phillipe did add that the first time they'd kissed was in Monte Carlo. They had climbed the stairs to the palace gardens and spent hours on a park bench looking over the sea.

"Shall we retire for a cognac?" the owner asked, licking his Partagas cigar. They all walked to the stern as the crew hopped to get snifters from the salon to the afterdeck.

"Why Cap-Ferrat?" asked the nosy Mrs. "Rotten-ham," as Michelle began thinking of her for her persistent frowning questioning. Michelle had let the cat out of the bag, with that comment during dinner, they'd been interested in settling there some day.

"Tomorrow we'll pass by there on the way to Monte Carlo and I will show you."

"Nonsense. Pass by? No chance. We're anchoring the west side, eh Captain?" the owner said as he overheard her answer.

"Wonderful idea, sir," Phillipe said.

"This cognac was made by an old friend of mine. It's almost like an Armanac. I think you'll like it," the owner said. It was quite remarkable to view the lights of Nice with such a fine snifter of cognac in hand.

Cap-Ferrat has anchorages on each side of its peninsula. The owner preferred the west-side mooring.

They arrived around three o'clock in the afternoon with full regalia and dropped the hook to be welcomed by one of the local fishermen. The cook quickly negotiated some fresh poissons for dinner. The dinghy was prepared for transporting the captain and Michelle, who would be ferried ashore by the young first mate as the others napped.

Phillipe and Michelle took a taxi alone to the home of a person they had known for years, Armand Arnoud. Armand knew the property there well and had often encouraged them to come and look. They felt comfortable to look at property with Armand because he knew of their means. Monsieur Armand had relations in the area for many years and knew which properties might be available long before most of the owners did. His talent was well noticed on the peninsula. His descriptions of the various seasons on the east beach, versus the plages west, were quite helpful to Michelle, who preferred the afternoon sun.

After tea at the Grand Hotel, where the concierge exchanged phone numbers to be helpful, they set out looking for a small plot of land on which they might one day consider building. Most of the neighbors in the area were part-time so it would make a very quiet home.

St. Tropez was a very busy little port then and their home would eventually fetch a fine price to go toward the building of a new estate.

"Ooh la la, c'est très . . ."

"Super, oui!" Armand said. The area had really become affluent since Michelle walked the beaches as a young cook ashore. She was so in love with the beauty that she could overlook the mansions poking through the cliffs, giving the owners a "vue du port." It was a beautiful site to build upon.

After discussing price, Michelle said quietly to her husband, "How could we possibly afford this now?" Armand overheard her. He was very accustomed to this reaction and with the calmest mannerisms said, "But of course it is expensive. This is an important feature! But, to attract people like yourselves, I am here to assist."

"What exactly does that mean?" Phillipe asked.

"Let me show to you a place you might enjoy," continued Armand. "To a small chateau near the beach!"

"But Armand, we could not possibly afford such a place now. We were in hopes of a place many years from now," Michelle said. The undeveloped site was too expensive for them, yet he was taking them to see a chateau. Their patience was on edge.

"Avec moi, s'il vous plait," Armand insisted. They drove into a secluded property with a short, beautiful gate and entry area. They could see a two-story dwelling through some trees and walked along limestone paths up to the house, which was scaled exactly to their expectations. The owner was Madame Cartas.

Phillipe and Michelle gravitated to the front lawn of the home as Armand announced their presence. Neither could speak because the place was perfect. Both were silently adding their worth, trying to figure how to afford it, without even knowing how enormous the price must be. Armand brought them inside while the Madame sat by a window staring at the glistening reflections. As they approached her, she asked them to sit. "Andreas told me you had already had your tea," she said. Andreas was the concierge they had just met. Phillipe and Michelle exchanged puzzled expressions.

"My husband was killed in the war. He was a captain, too," she said looking at Phillipe. "Been here since. My children worry about me falling off the cliffs—they should only worry that I jump," she said a bit too seriously. The small talk continued until Armand felt it was time to depart. "Please consider the place, not the price. Think about it overnight, and let's get together once again before you sail." He drove them to the dinghy and asked them to call on him for lunch the following day. Phillipe said he would weigh anchor at three o'clock in the afternoon, so they set time for an early lunch.

Once aboard, they discussed how much they loved the home and figured the absolute most they could pay. They told the story to the insistent Mrs. Rottingham. The eavesdropping owner felt they must be willing to pay much more.

The next morning they met Armand as planned. He drove them back to the hotel where there were a number of people waiting for them. Among them was Andreas, who took a seat at the corner sitting area where waiters busily hustled fresh prosciutto and melon with water as the group began to introduce themselves.

Monsieur Ranopolous—a lawyer, Monsieur Van de Veld—one of Madame Cartas' dearest friends. After brief food and conversation— and plenty of casual glances at each other—Phillipe said, "Michelle and I really appreciate you all being here. Yet, we feel we have intruded on your time because we come from such simple means than to even consider the affordability of such a beautiful home. After all, we came here only hoping to purchase a small plot to build on later in our lives."

After Phillipe finished his proclamation, the lawyer, Monsieur Ranopolous, began to speak in a very low voice while looking around at everyone. "I will like to tell you of a story." His heavy Greek Accent preferred English for delivery, although his French was acceptable. "And we speak with confidence only, no?" All nodded in agreement.

"You see, in 1610, a young Greek sailor named Rosseau came ashore here while the ship weathered bad winds. While ashore, he met Monsieur Rothschilde Maillot who lived very near here. For many years they visited each other, once in Greece at Mykonos where Rosseau lived with his ill mother. After she died, Rosseau goes to sailing and becomes a captain. Most of his trips were to the orient, and only occasionally near here. When Monsieur Maillot died, he left in his will his home to Rosseau. Ever since, this home has been handed down even to perfect strangers."

"Though various homes near Cap-Ferrat are rumored to have been a part of this tradition, Madame Cartas' home has been occupied since 1850, or so. Her husband was given the home from Captain Warren of Liverpool who got the place from Captain Parker of Southampton who acquired this property in exchange for the original property from Captain Richeau, the only Frenchman to have occupied this place in the 300 or so years since Maillot. That, basically, is it."

"We have records of all the owners and their histories, of course. The bank trust has only had to find one owner. That was in 1810 when the owner, Captain Severa, a Spaniard, and his wife were lost at sea on a voyage to America."

"Many of the wives, like Madam Cartas, have selected the recipient. She's ready to offer you this home. With all of its conditions, would you be kind enough to consider this your home? Your children, friends, etc. cannot know of this situation. This is the best-kept secret in the

Mediterranean and we believe it has roots from even more ancient times. Our records began in 1610 with a formal agreement, which we still have in our safekeeping. However, we have a letter written in Italian as translated from some Greek document that is missing. Some references predate by as many as 1,000 years because, oddly, the reference was from a fisherman with a very strong Christian heritage who talked to the Greeks about his home. Judging from the excerpts, which is all we can allow an outsider to see, it appears the original place was in St. Tropez."

With that Michelle gasped, "The tale by the sea!" Tears began to well in her eyes because of a famous tale told by the peasants to each other. She'd heard it from the nuns in her village teaching in church and once, as a young girl in St. Tropez while buying fish for her yacht, a crazy woman on the docks came up to her and said, "It's the tale of the seas!" and walked away. The tale was told to all youngsters that the sea could bring great riches if you worked hard and that a god of the sea would bestow a great shelter. It was assumed to be just a legend, since no one could ever prove the part about the shelter's existence.

"We couldn't possibly accept such an incredible honor," Phillipe said. "This is such an unreal experience to have the knowledge of this in itself. But we would never be worthy of . . . "

Andreas interrupted and said, "Yes, you're most definitely worthy. We have done our studies of you both, pardon our intrusion. Madame Michelle was born to a wonderful farming family and has provided for her siblings. You have four wonderful children. Captain Phillipe was the only child of a fishing family and worked his way through the ranks to be considered one of the most popular captains in the private fleet. In fact, we have hoped to entice you here for years and by chance, a few days ago, we found out you were coming when I overheard Armand. Today, as we mentioned, only we and Madame Cartas know of this. Last week, we let Armand in on it to ensure you could see the place properly."

Armand just nodded and then said, "This would be the greatest and most wonderful commission for me to have received," knowing the assignment meant no money ever exchanged hands.

Monsieur Van de Veld, dressed quite well, handled the affairs of Madame Cartas and had insisted he be included at the lunch. "I must apologize for my being here—I was only . . . "

"Never mind. You deserve to know, for your affection for the Madame. Your loyal services to her over the years are remarkable. We were to invite you anyway," Ranopolous said, fairly convincingly.

"Yes," said M. Ranopolous, "the house will be available in November. When the Madame moves to Crete to be with her daughter. No need to do anything but to sail to Greece, sign papers and view our file if you wish. We do prefer you move in by next summer if possible. You are, of course, held responsible to keep up the place, but know the repairs are covered by us through a trust, which I'm sure you might be happy to consider a contribution to when you have expired."

Aboard the *Hamptonesse*, Mrs. Rottingham started to inquire about the place. They smiled and said they had found the terms quite acceptable and gave her no more information. As they rounded the peninsula and looked up, the captain motioned for Ranopolous and Andreas. Madame Cartas was waving a handkerchief. The captain let the mighty horn of the yacht bellow across the waters with the puff of smoke that powered a blast rising above the *Hamptonesse* as she sailed away.

Is He Available?

"See you in the morning. I've got things to go do," Wally said as he picked up his briefcase and headed out of his office. Joyce, his assistant for the last five years, suspected he might be going down to the hospital where he volunteered a few hours here and there. She also knew that he preferred not to be questioned about his agenda.

It had been almost two months since Wally had put on his volunteer jacket and badge. Business had kept him from the hospital part of the time, but he had needed to take off a few weeks from the routine anyway. Patients who are not going to recover can take a toll on those who care for them. "The nursing staff in HIV wards are angels," Wally would say.

When Wally walked into the HIV section, the regular nursing staff acknowledged that they had missed him. "I've no real excuse," he said, "I'm just glad to be back." As he made his rounds, he confirmed what he already suspected—all new patients, except for one. Melvin Allen lay there under his tiger-skin-looking blanket, his head poking through the side of the bed guards.

"Help me sit up," he said to Wally. Wally tried to help him, but he could see the pain in Melvin's face and a nurse came in to help. Melvin looked happy to see Wally.

Wally sat down beside Melvin as the nurse rubbed lotion on Melvin's dry hands. "Can I have a ham and cheese sandwich?" Melvin asked. His frail body of bones told of weeks of malnutrition.

"I'll ask the supervisor to see what she can do," the nurse said, knowing this would be one of his last requests.

"I'll go see if I can get one downstairs," Wally said.

"You gonna buy him a sandwich?" the nurse asked with a curious, yet grateful, look.

"I don't mind," Wally answered as he headed down the stairs, knowing it would take hours any other way, to get him a sandwich. Fortunately, the little store had a ham and cheese sandwich.

"Here you go, Melvin," Wally said as he unwrapped the sandwich and broke off a very tiny piece. As he placed it in his mouth, the lengthy process of chewing began. Wally tried not to notice how long it was taking. "Do you like it?" he asked. Melvin nodded "yes," and when he finally swallowed he looked up and smiled to Wally.

"It's my favorite," he said.

The process of eating tiny pieces of the food, then drinking Shasta through a straw, went on for an hour. During that time, Wally looked at Melvin and asked, "Are you afraid to die?" "No," he shook his head. Wally acknowledged that with a smile. "Are you ready to die?" he asked, surprised at the frankness of his near-impossible question.

"Yes," he said.

Wally looked deep into his eyes and could see a sincere effort to communicate his willingness to die. He was ready to let go. Wally could tell the time had come, too.

"Melvin, they talk about a bright or white light . . . can you see it?"

Melvin closed his eyes and his lips said "Yes," but no sound emerged.

"Well, those are the angels coming for you," Wally said. "Go to them when you can. Pray for them to come to you. I'm praying too."

And Wally did pray as he held onto Melvin's bony arm. Melvin looked almost like he was dead for a brief minute, but then his eyes began to move underneath closed eyelids.

"Does it feel peaceful, Melvin?"

"Yes," he nodded.

"Then they are almost ready for you. Close your eyes and get some sleep tonight. If you wake up tomorrow, have them bring you another bite of the rest of your sandwich. You'll have that to look forward to. Then, just remember to trust the light and God will be ready for you."

After a silence Melvin once again looked deep into Wally's eyes and then his silent lips asked another question.

"What's that, Melvin? I can't hear you."

He looked again deeply at Wally and vocalized, "Is he available?"

Wally paused to ponder what Melvin was asking.

"Is he available?" Wally said, checking to see if he had heard correctly.

Melvin responded firmly, "Yes. Is he available?"

"God?" Wally asked.

Melvin looked relieved and said "Yes."

Not sure why or where this question was coming from, Wally said, "Yes. He is. The Bible says that if you ask forgiveness for your sins, you'll have life everlasting. Do you understand that?"

Melvin nodded.

"God is available for you. And, tell Him hello for me when you see Him! In fact, whenever I get to heaven, I hope you'll look me up." With that, Melvin closed his eyes. Wally placed his hand on the side of Melvin's head and said, "I love you, Melvin."

The next morning, Wally was on a plane to Las Vegas to meet friends for a bachelor party. Not being a sophisticated gambler, Wally chose to use wagers far short of his means. This kept it fun and interesting, but not businesslike.

Walking past the roulette wheel, Wally wondered if there was a way to bet with Melvin in mind. The only idea he could think of was the number 26, Melvin's room number. Number 26 was a black number. Melvin was a black man. As he watched, without betting, 26 black was the number.

Curious of the coincidence, the next mental list came to Wally when he sat with his friends at the blackjack table. His instincts won over reason several times and paid off. Once he looked at the card in his hold, a five, and wished to be dealt a six. Six came next. Later, he added incorrectly and thought eight was the card he needed when, in fact, a seven would produce 21. An eight appeared.

Early the next morning, Wally called the nursing station and received confirmation that Melvin had left the world Friday night. Saddened a bit but happy, too, Wally said a short prayer for him.

Saturday night the casino was alive. Wally wagered $10 to $20 a roll on the dice table and figured out it wasn't a good night for the throwers.

He bet the "don't pass" line and did very well, but lost as the numbers he placed side bets on cost him when the roller crapped out.

The pit boss raised the minimum bet from $5 to $10. A new roller's seven out of the shoot alerted Wally that the table might be warming up. So, he threw a $5 chip down on the field. The stick man tapped his chip and said a bit rudely "$10, sir." Wally looked at him, puzzled. He looked squarely at the pit boss—he'd been betting well above the minimum for quite a while, yet they chose to treat him a bit harshly.

Wally said to the pit boss, "How about raising the maximum bet from two to four thousand? Fair is fair."

The pit boss looked stern and unimpressed. He said, "Sir, you can read as well as I what the limits are on the table."

Wally reached in his pocked and threw out a number—a marker for $15,000. "Five-hundred-dollar chips, please," Wally said. As they struggled to put together the chips, excitement and confusion wrestled around the table.

Wally pointed demandingly at the pit boss and the overhead camera and said, "Sir, I have been a gentleman up to this point in not addressing the fact that this is one of the coldest crap tables I've ever seen." And with that he placed $2,000 on "don't pass." The rollout number was five and, several rolls later, he was a winner.

As the tense game continued he won and lost a couple but was still up $2,000 when the shooter threw a double six, or "box cars." "Oh, well what have we here?" Wally said. "Let's see if he can do it again," he said, tossing a thousand onto the double six. That roll was an eight, a loser on the bet, which pays 30-to-one. He threw another thousand out, still keeping his $2,000 on *don't pass*. He wasn't sure if he was breaking the rules, but they took his money again when the shooter threw a six. "Halfway is a good sign," he declared and threw out $1,500 on the double six. "Here we go, Melvin," he mumbled. The table erupted in noise when he hit, and the table attendant scurried to arrange the $45,000 win.

"How about raising the limit?" Wally asked the overhead cameras. He shifted his eyes to the pit boss. "Yes, sir," he said as they raised the limit to $10,000. By this time there was a crowd three deep around the table. Wally's luck continued as he kept placing $5,000 on "don't pass" and roller after roller eventually crapped out.

"How much am I up?" Wally asked his attendant.

"You're doing well, sir." They changed the guard at the table.

"Get me a number," he said knowing they were keeping track upstairs. Several rolls later, they sent word he was up $85,000.

He placed $10,000 on "don't pass" and won. The pit boss had sweat on his head and the anxiety behind the table was intense. Something told Wally to table one more stab at the casino. "Tell you what, sir," he said. "What's your name?"

The pit boss responded, "Anthony Thomas, sir."

Wally continued, "I'll leave right now if you give each of the people at this table $300."

"Sir, I can't do that," said Anthony Thomas. Wally put $10,000 on "don't pass." The rolls proclaimed another winner, with his earnings now over $100,000. "OK, sir," said Anthony, "Why don't you go relax with your winnings and we'll honor your request for the other rollers."

"Thank you, sir, but now that'll be six hundred each," said Wally. The table cheered. The pit boss didn't wait for a decision from upstairs to acquiesce.

Looking up, but not at the camera, Wally said, "Thanks, Mr. Allen. I'm glad you were available."

Down on the Dog

Subsurface aquatic species lurch below. Depends on where you are and what time of year. In this place of dreams there live mullet, bream, green trout, catfish and eels.

Occasionally, sheepshead, red fish and drum. Croakers are everywhere, not sure why they croak. Specs are there, they don't croak. They eat good and croakers don't.

Alligators used to live here. So did the amazing alligator gar, a weird looking fish that gets big when not bothered. Gar fishing rodeos wiped out most of the big ones; fishermen competing to hang 'um high. Speedboats got the rest.

Rare are the dolphin and the tarpon, but they visit here too. Surely a shark finds it's way as well—it'd be silly to think not. The wind blows up the brackish muddy water aroma. The calm accentuates other smells closed eyes would always recognize. Close your eyes and see if you can smell it. Gosh how it reminds you to honor the nose for its memory.

Turtles usually jump off logs when you approach. Sometimes, they don't. Trees overhang the edge of the water unless there is a marsh thick with reeds pointing upward. All kinds of stuff goes on in that marsh.

Crabs walk slowly under the water, while a dog's bark easily travels over it. Boathouses built of cypress, their boats of mahogany. Their captains built of passion, their guests of faith.

Take a picnic down on the wharf, dangle your feet in the water, sip something cool, turn up the music, or not. The seagull's successes are pleasing to watch and the grass is growing so fast it'll be time to do chores again soon, but an afternoon sail will get in the way of yard work.

Ready about, hard alee!

Abigail's Fairy Tale

Once upon a time, in a beautiful field of daisies with very colorful blooms of yellow and purple, a little girl played with her friends. Her name was Margole and she had long, curly blonde hair. Fluffy, tall grasses helped make the ground soft and the children enjoyed the cushion when they fell down. Nearby was a cottage painted white with dark-green shutters.

Gusts of wind would cause all of those beautiful things growing in the fields to sway back and forth, making the breezes almost visible. The motion of the blooms gave the children something to watch when they took a break from their games.

Margole liked the magic of wild daisies dancing. She would speak to them and they always seemed to answer her. One day, a storm was brewing and the sky turned a scary, dirty green. Margole kept playing, unaware that a thunderstorm, or even a tornado, might be approaching. Little girls don't know much about the dangers of Mother Nature, but as the sky turned darker, the sound of thunder could be heard. A shout from her mother and in an instant, they all were safely in the underground cellar. This place provided storage for potatoes, onions and her father's favorite Bordeaux wine. Not much happened on the farm this time, but the thought of that dangerous wind was something Margole would not forget. She asked her mother what happened to the birds in a bad storm and wished for them to be safe. She thought about how nice it would be to fly as a bird over the fields of flowers. That's when something very strange happened. The beautiful daisies lifted her up, suspended in air, and the next thing you knew she was flying above the field and around her house. How nice would it be to fly over to her friend Sheila's house and see if she was out riding her horse, Freeborn. Then, maybe she'd fly away to see the world.

Her arms were moving up and down. Her wings were big and colorful. "My goodness," she thought, "I'm flying!"

The flight that first day took Margole around the fields and she headed over to see her father's rose garden. Soon, after landing on a white rose bloom, she took off again to see the world.

After two days of flying, she landed on a fence to rest, when she realized it was the fence on her friend's horse farm. A dove landed near her and they began to talk. The dove started to laugh when Margole began complaining about how long she had been flying, yet how little distance she had traveled. "You're a butterfly!" he said. "Butterflies usually don't fly very far." A butterfly? She'd never thought about becoming a slow-flying erratic butterfly. She was still pouting at the thought of that when the dove said, "Yes, but look how beautiful you are!"

"My gosh!" she said. "I am beautiful!" So, up and away she flew, out into the open fields where the wind would blow her around and there were plenty of flowers to land upon. On her journey, she met bumblebees and lightning bugs. They all said how pretty she was. And she always said just how pretty they were, too. She even met a little green frog jumping from one blade of grass to another. His real name was Gonhoppinston, but everyone just called him Froggie. Froggie liked Margole, and he affectionately called her Madame Margole. He had been jumping along for a year and had only traveled about one mile. He wished he could fly like she could. They talked all night and, at daylight, Froggie went looking for some breakfast and Madame Margole flew away to see the world.

That night she met Alfred the cricket. Alfred would chirp awhile, then he would talk awhile. She found out that a big green trout had almost eaten up Alfred when he accidentally fell into a pond. Margole was laughing at Alfred because he was funny, saying "No big ol' trout's gonna like Mr. Alfred chirping away in their tummy!" Margole took a nap and Alfred kept on chirping, until daylight when she took off once again to see the world.

Margole had a big breeze lift her high above the treetops the next day and she could see forever. With those strong winds, she began to realize she had traveled a long distance. Finally, she landed upon an old fence with rusty wire. There was a dusty dirt road on one side and cows on the other side and she watched the cows flicking their tails at flies. Birds with long legs were all around them and even landed atop of the cows' backs. She'd never watched the birds and the cows before.

The next day, she would lift off to fly away again to see the world.

Landing in the backyard of a little house scattered with plastic toys, she wondered how many children lived here. She was just about to fly away when a cute little boy came running outside. Then, out came a little girl who looked to be just a little older than the little boy. They liked to play with each other and the silly little boy made the girl laugh.

Margole heard someone calling for Abby. She looked up and there was that little boy standing next to her bed with a donut. She was not a butterfly anymore, just a little girl again with the rest of her life to fly away and see the world!

Margole's Maiden Voyage

The beautiful passenger ship SS *Copa Cabanana* was tied up to the docks at the end of Government Street in downtown Mobile. The hull was painted a dark beautiful blue, and the white color of the upper decks gave the ship a very dressed-up look. The passengers were boarding. Margole was one of them, wearing a khaki dress and her favorite yellow hat. The porter had taken her suitcase already, so all she had to deal with was her rather large personal bag, which contained a couple of magazines and several books her teacher had selected for her to read while on her voyage.

The big engines of the ship, with the black and gray smoke coming out of the smokestack, were powered by steam. The sounds and smells of a large ship preparing to cast off were so exciting for her to experience. This would be her first journey at sea and the fact that she was still just a little girl didn't affect her enthusiasm a bit. Her family had given her permission to go on the ship, destination Cape St. Banana. She had heard captivating stories of beautiful beaches, sugar cane plantations with big porches, fresh fruit growing everywhere, excursions inland to see tropical rain forests and small settlements of people who created beautiful crafts from the various items found in their lush environment.

Margole received special attention as she boarded. After all, she was a beautiful little girl with a yellow hat. Several members of the ship's crew greeted her, showed her to her cabin and introduced her to her roommate for the voyage, a girl named Pricilla. They were the same age and became fast friends. Travel time to the Cape was estimated to be about 10 days, so there would be plenty of time for the girls to meet some of the other children on the SS *Copa Cabanana*. Margole had also packed plenty of art supplies for the trip and she and Pricilla planned to create a few masterpieces. Pricilla's Aunt Grace was an accomplished artist and had paid for Pricilla to be onboard for this inaugural journey to the land of inspiration. Aunt Grace was ill now and could not make the voyage with her.

Cape St. Banana, a magical barrier island rich with history, awaited their arrival!

The *Copa Cabanana* was once one of the finer ships in the world and had successfully made many worthy excursions in her time. She had sailed all around the globe, but this would be the first time the ship would visit Cape St. Banana. The crew members were excited to be going there too, for many stories existed telling of the most enriched experiences there.

The ship was gracefully pulled from the pier by a couple of little tugboats late in the afternoon. Three blasts of the ship's horn announced their departure, of which the girls had been forewarned. Had they not been warned, they would surely have been much more startled by the loud noise. The girls were off to the railing to watch the waterfront as the ship moved slowly southerly towards Mobile Bay. The shipyard they passed was full of ships in for repairs. A big ship completely out of the water was quite a sight to see for the first time. The girls learned the wing wall of the dry dock was flooded to make it sink. The vessel was then floated over the dock. Once in place, the water was pumped out of the intentionally sunken dock leaving the ship high and dry, resting on blocks of wood. Steam cranes moved welding machines around, and welders torches sparked as they replaced the worn-out steel.

"And that pile of stuff is called bauxite," a voice said. The girls turned to see a crew member standing there with his white clothing and a little blue sailor cap on his head.

"What do they do with it?" Pricilla asked.

"I'm not sure, but I'll ask," he said. "My name is Pete, by the way." The girls said hello to Pete and watched the ship passing in between the red and green buoys and into the bay.

They could see Montrose on the eastern shore with its big red clay cliff, and then saw someone pointing to a bridge on the other side of the bay. Margole overheard them say that it was at the mouth of Dog River. Pricilla's aunt grew up near that river as a child and told stories of going to the Alba Club on the weekends to swim and sail. "She always talked about the hamburgers there," Pricilla recalled.

"Pete, what's that?" Margole asked.

"That's called 'middle bay light.' It used to have a big light on it so ships could navigate better at night. Today, with all of the channel marked like it is, they don't use it anymore."

"It sure looks like they use it," she said.

"Yes, they just painted it. Seems that some of the locals found some money to help keep it up. I've never seen another like it. I'm glad they didn't tear it down," Pete said, making a point to the young girls that it is only kept up for the sake of history. The crew of the SS *Copa Cabanana* were remarkably very well trained, almost like teachers, for the younger passengers experiencing so much for the first time. "Once we get to the mouth of the bay, you will see a Civil War fort on each side of us. The one on our left, or our port side, is Fort Morgan. The one to our right, our starboard side, is Fort Gaines. This is where Admiral Farragut said, "Gosh those torpedoes, full speed ahead!" Pete exclaimed. "His boat, called an ironclad and named the Tecumseh, is still sitting at the bottom of the bay from hitting one!" he said with a little chuckle.

Once offshore, the sight of the beach fading away in the dark, the girls were escorted to the dining area for their first meal. The dining area was paneled with beautiful varnished wood and the long tables had white tablecloths. They were seated with several other younger children who were each with one of their parents. Chuck, a little freckle-faced boy from Demopolis, Alabama, was there with his mother, and Tommy was there with his grandfather, a doctor from New Orleans. Tommy was doing a good job making sure everyone knew he was funny, and his grandfather was enjoying watching him. The boys were 10 years old, a little older than the girls. Dinner was brought to the table family style . . . fried chicken, mashed potatoes, collards and biscuits. The doctor made a comment about their not wanting to send the passengers, mostly Southerners, into shock by serving tropical food the first night. Dessert was a big bowl of ice cream and cookies and the children began to wander around as the adults enjoyed some coffee.

The routine over the next 10 days was to eat breakfast, then the children went to an orientation at various times in the auditorium (which also served as a movie theater at night). They learned all about how Cape St. Banana was first sighted by the Spaniards as they passed by, not realizing it held such magical charm or that it was an island. All they could see was a long spit of land and banana trees, hence the name. Over a hundred years later, an explorer named Olsen from Norway decided to check it out. There were large turtles swimming in the protected harbor, porpoises escorting the ship in and beautiful large birds flying over the palms. The crew found abundant fresh water and fruit— a blessing, since they were running low. They saw a large hill in the distance and, when they began the trek up the hill, they found the remains of an ancient settlement.

Margole asked, "Where did the people go?"

The teacher responded, "We don't know for sure. From the records Captain Olsen made, it appears they just left since everything like their cooking utensils were still neatly stored. We don't know where they went, but they seemed to have everything they would have needed to stay."

The crew had spent six months there, mapping the island, and staking a claim. They left several willing crew members on the island and sailed back to Norway to tell of their find. While they were gone, the new settlers began to build homes and plant vegetables. Over the next several years, ships from all over the world visited them. Each time, a few crew members or passengers would buy parcels of property from the Norwegians and settle there, too.

Captain Cook went about exploring other parts of the world, and Cape St. Banana was forgotten. That is until recently, when a famous Hollywood actress, Tula Tunnel, bought a large plantation and threw her 60th birthday party on the Cape. Her friends stayed with the locals, since there were no hotels.

There are still no hotels—that's why passengers stayed aboard the ship. The SS *Copa Cabanana* was a large ship, but she nestled into the quaint harbor just fine. From there, a launch took passengers to the island and back, during the day.

Chuck and his mother joined Margole for a movie the night before they arrived in Cape St. Banana. The movie was called "It's a Mad,

Mad, Mad, Mad World," and it was very funny. They all laughed a lot. After the movie, they went to bed knowing they would awaken anchored at Cape St. Banana.

Tommy's grandfather knocked on Margole and Pricilla's cabin door. "You girls want to join me on deck to see the island?"

"Sure!" he heard and out they came in a flash. They walked to the stairs, taking their time as the aged doctor slowly ascended behind them. Tommy was already on deck. They could hear voices of other passengers and the excitement of the morning was felt throughout the ship. Once outside, they were very excited. Banana trees, palm trees, white sand beaches, clear blue water, warm breezes, sea birds and cute cottages lining the edge of the harbor were amazing sights to behold.

"I'm going to have fun here," Pricilla said.

"Me too," the doctor said.

They stayed in the harbor for three days. Each day there were different excursions around the island. Margole drew sketches of trees, cottages and the ship as it lay at anchor. Tommy and Chuck were always swimming and watching the local fishermen catch fish off the beach. Everyone bought beads to wear and take home to their family and friends. The beautiful coral stone necklaces and bracelets, along with earrings, made shopping a lot of fun. The prices were very reasonable for the children as they could buy for half price. Local teachers would hold classes after lunch for them, telling stories of the rich history of the island, forgotten by the Spaniards who never stopped, and then by the rest of the world who were always looking for somewhere else. Margole could not understand how any other place could be prettier. "Nor can I," the doctor said, "and I've seen most of them."

Margole grew up with the magical memories of Cape St. Banana. Her favorite sketch hangs framed in her room at home. It's of one of the plantation homes overlooking the harbor; the smokestack of the SS *Copa Cabanana* is visible just above the palm trees.

One day, Margole dreams of bringing her children to see this magical place.

The beautiful sketch never left the wall of Margole's home and, with the promised magic of Cape St. Banana, those experiences and friends did last for their lifetimes.

Out to Sea

A day will come for us, when tomorrow will not.

The end of a full life begins with enriched remembrance of our voyage. A chart of the ocean brilliantly shows off the way things were, guiding us through the perils we faced, enabling the enjoyment we reaped.

Gone are our thoughts that never emerged.

Deep emotions, safely locked inside us. Oh, the ease of inhibited expression tightly lashed to the gunnel so secure. Far out at sea, the falling of tides doesn't matter.

The ocean can suppress the selfishness of complacency by delivering great humbleness.

Unfair are the intentionally unexplored harbors. Given fair winds you can sail through life without much thought about what might be somewhere, avoiding potential risks. The fare of that sort of excursion can be extraordinary when you reflect on your entire journey.

Wonderful are our words and actions that make up our now-charted sea of life, beautifully decorated with our final sunset.

Incredible are the little splashes of respect on our decks as others, preparing our perfect voyage to beyond the last buoy, swab them with eulogy. The sea buoy bows, flashing and moaning, on our passing.

The compass has no meaning anymore. The weather doesn't either. You navigate in the stars, not by them. Your omniscient captain of this eternal voyage uncleats your soul from any remaining burdens. Finally, you are free to be you.

ABOUT THE AUTHOR

Bobbo Jetmundsen was born in Mobile, Alabama. He attended two different public high schools as court ordered desegregation was imposed during his tenure. He was a student at Davidson High School for two years, then graduated from Murphy High School in 1973, where he was active in student government. He served as President of the Pan Hellenic Council (governing all local fraternities and sororities) of the famous Mobile High School Greek System and was a member of the Phi Kappa fraternity.

The Mobile Bay area provided ample opportunity for sailing, hunting, fishing and inspiration for some of his short stories. His mother still lives there, along with many of his friends.

Bobbo attended Rhodes College in Memphis, Tennessee, where he also was active in student activities as Vice President of the Student Body, President of the Student Center and active in the Sigma Alpha Epsilon fraternity. Bobbo attributes the landscape of this small liberal arts college for introducing him to writing short stories and adequately filling his head with memories and experiences. He graduated with a B.A. in Economics and a B.A. in Political Science in 1977. He currently serves on the Rhodes College Alumni Board.

After college, Bobbo worked in Mobile for the Alabama Dry Dock and Shipbuilding Company as the assistant to the Vice President of Sales for two years, when he was recruited to the same position with Jacksonville Shipyards in Jacksonville, Florida, where he stayed for less than two years. This short career, nonetheless, had a significant impact on Bobbo and he still considers those experiences in the marine industry irreplaceable.

Just as the bull market of the 1980s began, Bobbo shifted careers and joined Merrill Lynch and Co. in Atlanta, Georgia, as a stockbroker. In 1985, he moved to Morgan Keegan and Company, where he still works today as a Managing Director. He serves on various boards of directors and advisors for early-stage companies, and is considered an active "angel investor."

Bobbo lives in the historic Ansley Park neighborhood of Atlanta and travels extensively in the Southeast. He has been a private pilot since he was in college and is currently flying his second airplane made by the Mooney Aircraft Company.

Give the Gift of
RAINING RUM
to Your Friends and Colleagues

CHECK YOUR LEADING BOOKSTORE OR ORDER HERE

❑ **YES,** I want _____ copies of *Raining Rum* at $22.95 each, plus $4.95 shipping per book (GA residents please add $1.61 sales tax per book). Canadian orders must be accompanied by a postal money order in U.S. funds. Allow 15 days for delivery.

❑ **YES,** I am interested in having Bobbo Jetmundsen speak or give a seminar to my company, association, school or organization. Please send information.

My check or money order for $_____ is enclosed.

Please charge my ❑ Visa ❑ MasterCard ❑ Discover ❑ American Express

Name _____

Organization _____

Address _____

City/State/Zip _____

Phone_____ E-mail_____

Card # _____

Exp. Date_____ Signature _____

Please make your check payable and return to:
Bobbo Publishing
P.O. Box 550028
Atlanta, GA 30355
www.rainingrum.com